Cherry

Annie Seaton

Pentecost Island 6

DEDICATION

For those women who struggle with self-confidence.

Know you are a unique individual and let your own light shine.

Prologue

Pippa

Saturday night in the Turtle Bar on Pentecost Island was shaping up to be a big night. The girls had decided to throw a pre-wedding party for Rafe and I—two weeks before our upcoming wedding—as well as a belated—by eight years— wedding celebration for Evie and Jed. It was a sit-down dinner in the bar, and I knew it was going to be really hard for Tamsin to let go of her kitchen to the new chef, but we'd all insisted that she put the new sous chef, Angus Alexander, in charge for the night.

'You don't have to do this for us,' Evie said when we told her. Jed had barely left her side since they'd arrived three days ago. I'll never forget the feeling of joy that filled me when I waited on the wharf with Tamsin on Tuesday afternoon for Evie to arrive on Jiminy's boat with three other guests, as well as Angus. Evie and Jed had got back together last month when Evie had gone down to Brisbane to be a bone marrow donor for her brother.

Over the months she had worked as the

landscaper at Ma Carmichael's Resort, Evie had become one of us. My aunt had left me the house and land on the island, and the new resort was well under development.

'Oh yes, we do,' I replied. 'There's a lot to celebrate and you belong to the island, Evie. You are a part of us and you always will be, even after you move to Brisbane with Jed.' Evie had agreed to stay on while the building work was being done and I advertised for a new landscaper; she seemed really excited about moving back to Brisbane with Jed.

Seeing Evie in her husband's arms as the boat came into the bay was a very happy moment for me—one of the many highlights of our time on the island.

If anyone deserved happiness, it was Evie, and I'll never forget the look on her face when I told her that she and Jed were booked into one of the new huts for a week's honeymoon as a belated wedding present from the girls. After that, they would stay in her small room at the back of the house. Jed wasn't keen—yet—about staying on Evie's boat, *Kestrel*, but I knew she'd convince him in the end.

Evie was a different person to the tense woman who'd left Pentecost Island to go down to Brisbane to see if she was a bone marrow match for her brother, Zeke. We'd all been so happy for them when the operation had been a success and Zeke had made a good recovery.

Tonight was going to be a night for celebration: our upcoming wedding, Evie and Jed's reconciliation and the progress of the resort, which was steaming ahead at a great rate, thanks to the wonderful Riccardo brothers.

The lights were already on around the bar when Rafe and I strolled down after sunset.

'You never considered calling this the "Happy Ever After Resort", did you?' Rafe commented as we walked, his arm around my shoulders.

'We did toss around a lot of ideas. But it *was* before the happy-ever-afters began.'

He pulled me closer and brushed his lips across my cheek. I stopped walking, turned and reached up to kiss his mouth. 'And there've been a few of them lately, haven't there?' he said.

I nodded. Rafe and I, Eliza and Phillipe, Nell and Nat, Tamsin and Gabe, and now Evie and Jed. 'Maybe we *should* have named the resort something with "happy" in it,' I said.

'I do like "Ma Carmichael's" though,' he said. 'And it makes your Aunty Vi a part of the place.'

I would be forever thankful to Aunty Vi for selling half of the island to Rafe, and leaving the rest to me.

Rafe and I had both dressed up in honour of the celebrations, and when we walked in, I was pleased to see we weren't the only ones who'd made an effort. The bar tables, covered with our new white tablecloths had been pulled into a U-shape so we could all talk easily to each other. Vibrant tropical flowers filled small glass vases and the new cutlery and glassware shone in the soft candlelight.

Sienna and Eliza were wearing colourful dresses, and they each had a hibiscus flower tucked into their hair. Another surge of happiness ran through me as I thought about how my life had changed; I loved my island, and I loved my friends—both old and new—and I loved the man by my side.

I stood on my toes and reached up and brushed another kiss across Rafe's lips. 'Have I told you I love you today?'

Rafe raised one elegant finger and placed it on his cheek as he tipped his head to the side. Dark eyes gleamed with laughter and his beautiful face creased in a smile. 'Yes, I believe you have. Have I told you how gorgeous you look tonight?'

I smiled back at him and smoothed my hands down the sides of the pale blue silk dress that I'd found in a new boutique on Hamilton Island last week. The silk whispered against my bare legs when I moved.

'You did. And you don't look half-bad yourself, but you could have tried harder, boyo. Look, Phillipe is wearing a tux.'

Rafe chuckled. 'He is, but at least I have shoes on.'

I giggled as I looked at the handsome Frenchman's tanned, but bare, feet. 'He might be quiet, but I think Phillipe is a bit of a rogue,' I whispered.

'I'm sure he is,' Rafe agreed.

Nat and Gabe were deep in conversation across the bar. Nat grinned and held up a bottle of bubbles as I walked over.

'Of course. I hope you two aren't talking work.' I smiled and looked around. 'Where're the girls?'

Nat chuckled and Gabe shook his head and pointed towards the house.

'Where do you think?' he said. 'Nell's in the office and Tam's gone to the kitchen. We both have workaholic partners.'

'You've created monsters, Pippa,' Nat said.

I rolled my eyes. 'They're both supposed to be off duty! That's why Angus came over earlier in the week, and why I've got Mirabelle working as waitress, and Tess in the office. I know that Jiminy was late bringing Cherry over, but Tam doesn't need to be in the kitchen at all. Or Nell in the office! I'll go and hurry them up.'

Our pool of available casual staff was building nicely, and we'd been able to hire some top notch staff. Ma Carmichael's was growing faster than we'd ever imagined, thanks to Eliza's partnership and financial contribution.

Sienna and Eliza were talking to one of the couples staying on the island. Dinner for the guests was being served on the veranda of the house, but we'd left the bar open for pre-dinner drinks for those who wanted to call in. Being Saturday night, as usual we had a few of the yachties in for a drink and finger food. The buzz of conversation and laughter added to the vibe.

'Any orders for the kitchen, Nat?'

'Yes, please.' He handed me a page from the docket book.

'Thanks.' I paused on the way out and smiled at the older couple sitting at the end of the bar. 'Welcome to Ma Carmichael's.' After a brief chat, I turned to Sienna and Eliza and spoke quietly. 'You both look gorgeous.'

'So do you, love,' Eliza said as she gestured to my dress. 'Stunning.'

'I'm happy with it.'

'I can't wait to see the wedding dress,' Eliza

replied. 'I think you're mean not to show us.'

'It's a surprise for everyone,' I said. I'd fallen in love with the unusual dress the instant I'd seen it in the same boutique last week. I'd left my run so late, I'd been starting to worry that I wasn't going to find anything suitable.

'Where are you off to now?' Sienna asked.

'The house. I won't be long.' I shook my head with a wry smile. 'I'm going over to hurry up the workaholics. I hope Tam and Nell are dressed for the occasion.'

'They are. They called in here before Nell went to the office and Tam went to meet the boat.' Eliza lifted her glass. 'They both had a quick glass of bubbles here first. Why don't you have one before you go up?'

'Thanks, but I'll go over and drag them back.' I rolled my eyes and headed to the house.

It was a beautiful, clear night and the moon was high in a brilliant star-studded sky. The water shone silver under the bright moon, and the gentle sounds of the waves pushing up the shingled sand provided a soothing backdrop. The solar lights in Evie's gardens were directed up towards the huts, and they looked welcoming in the soft light. The whole place was starting to get a feel of its own and the word that came to my mind was "classy".

Casual, but yes, classy. Since Eliza had

come in as a financial partner, we'd purchased a higher end of fittings and furniture than we thought we'd be able to afford, and the resort looked great.

Happiness trickled through me as I compared what I was seeing now to what Pentecost Island had looked like on our arrival almost a year ago.

We've done well, I thought as I walked along the paved path to the original house where I'd lived with Tam and Nell when we'd first moved to the island. The kitchen was still in use, but not for much longer; the commercial kitchen was almost ready—we were waiting for the installation of the gas cooktop and ovens and I was really hoping that it would be finished for our wedding on Saturday week. The new kitchen was near the bar, and the outdoor restaurant was almost finished too. The Riccardo Brothers, the building company I had engaged, had worked like Trojans, and hopefully this would be the last few days that the kitchen in the house would be used for a large group. We had taken over the bar for our celebration tonight, but had left the bay side of the bar open for the yachtie crowd; some of the regulars were propping up the bar across from our table.

The new setup was very different to the days when Aunty Vi had catered for guests in the old house. At least it had meant that there was room for the staff to live—so far, albeit in very close quarters. If things went to plan, I was going to build some staff accommodation up the hill away from the huts in the next development stage.

As I walked up the steps I frowned. Loud voices were coming from the kitchen, but I detoured across to the couple who were already seated at the table overlooking the bay.

'Hello, I hope you enjoy your dinner. Mr and Mrs Clarke, isn't it?'

'Yes, but Jeff and Dianne, please.' The young woman gestured to the bay where the moonlight had lit the water to incandescent silver. The occasional bird call provided a natural soundtrack to the dining area. 'We love your resort. With a view like this, the food doesn't matter.'

'We've already posted some of our photos on Instagram, and the posts have already had a couple of hundred likes,' Jeff said.

'Thank you. Word of mouth is the best—' I cut off as Cherry's voice, shrill and at full volume broke the quiet.

'No way!'

'Please excuse me,' I said with a tight smile and hurried along the veranda to the door that led to the kitchen.

'I will not work under this . . . this . . . monster. If I'd known you were going to be here,

Angus Alexander, I would have run a mile.' Cherry Chilcott had first worked for us on the official bar opening, and as well as showing what a great worker she was that night, Tam also knew her from a restaurant on the Gold Coast where she'd worked as a cocktail waitress. When I'd interviewed Cherry on Hamilton Island a few weeks ago, she told me she was equally experienced as a kitchen hand, and that she preferred to work with food rather than beverage. I knew Tam was impressed and was hoping to offer her a traineeship if that was the case.

As I stepped into the kitchen, Tamsin's soft, calm voice was drowned out by the words of Angus, the new chef.

'If I'd known that this incompetent, lazy, dishonest woman was on the island, I would have packed my bags and run as fast and far as I could,' his deep voice boomed.

I widened my eyes and stopped dead in the doorway. Our new chef was holding a huge knife and pointing it at Cherry.

'Look at him, this is assault,' Cherry screeched. 'He's threatening me with a knife.'

'Listen to her! Where's the quiet, shy Cherry gone now? All an act!' Angus yelled. 'Can't help yourself, can you?'

'Oh, for goodness sake, both of you.' Tam had to yell to be heard over the angry voices.

'Would you please calm down!'

I stepped into the room unnoticed, pulled a saucepan off the hook above the countertop and banged it on the bench. Once, but hard.

There was instant silence after the sound reverberated through the kitchen and everyone turned to look at me.

'Immediately,' I said, keeping my voice low, calm and controlled, even though I felt like screeching too. I was horrified by the behaviour in the kitchen. 'Do you realise there are guests on the veranda who can hear every word coming from this kitchen? Cherry, stop yelling. Angus, put that knife down immediately. Mirabelle, please take a complimentary bottle of wine to the Clarke couple sitting at the table at the corner of the veranda. Tell them I'll talk to them on my way out. Here's an order to put up too.' I handed the order to Mirabelle and waited until she'd put it up above the benchtop.

Three faces, one exasperated and two angry and flushed, turned to look at me.

'Now just what the hell is going on in my resort?' I asked coldly.

Chapter One

Cherry

When Cherry Chilcott stepped onto the wharf at Ma Carmichael's resort knowing that this time she was here to stay *and* had a permanent job, excitement zinged through her, despite her worry about being late on her first day of permanent work. Jiminy's launch had been delayed coming across from Hamilton Island, and Tamsin Jones had been waiting at the jetty for her.

'Sorry, we were late getting away,' Cherry apologised as they hurried along the path towards the house.

'All good. There's plenty of time before dinner. I wanted to ask you a couple of things. Do you mind if we chat as we walk?' Tamsin asked.

'Sure. What's up?'

'I know you have a great work ethic, Cherry. I remember the hours you used to put in at the bar at Surfside when we worked there together. Pippa said that you wanted to be in the food side of things. I didn't know that. I always thought you were making a career in the bar, and wanting to get into entertainment.'

'Oh no. Never entertainment.' Cherry shook

her head.

'You have such a fun personality and vivacious manner, I'm sure most of the patrons came back to watch—and hear—you make the cocktails. It was the entertainment, not the cocktails, that were the attraction.'

'Yep, that was me. The singing cocktail girl.' Cherry chuckled and shook her head. 'That was the "work" me. You'd be surprised if you knew how shy I really am. There's no way I could do it as a career. If it helps me keep a job though, I can put it on for a short time.'

'Well, you did it very well. And boy, you can sing. I heard you sing that *Kokomo* song from the *Cocktail* movie. You were as good as the Beach Boys!'

Cherry's face heated with embarrassment. 'Thank you, but I'm not really that good.'

'You are. Now tell me before we get to the house, if you really do have an interest in being a chef.'

'Oh yes.' Cherry widened her eyes trying to get her enthusiasm across. 'I've always had a passion for food and cooking. I really didn't have any other talents as I grew up. I hated school, I didn't play any sport, and I wasn't really good at anything—apart from singing— but I soon found if I followed a recipe I could get a result.'

What she didn't add was that it was one of the few things that didn't lead to constant criticism from her father. She knew he enjoyed her cooking, even though he never once told her. Being the middle child, with an older brother who was really clever, and always at the top of his class, and a younger sister who played representative netball, touch football and hockey, Cherry had been used to the not measuring-up comments for most of her life.

It had been easier to withdraw into herself, nod and smile, and spend her teenage weekends in the kitchen. Byron would be in his room swotting up for the next exam, and Leanne would be out playing a game somewhere with Mum and Dad traipsing around the countryside behind her. And when there was no one there, she could sing to her heart's content. Byron couldn't hear her; he always had his headphones on listening to music while he studied.

Cherry's self-confidence had taken a beating over the years, but she'd learned to hide that behind a brash and sassy personality in the workplace.

'You've got great people skills,' Tamsin continued. 'And that's what I'm looking for. And I've seen you work in a team.'

Great people skills? If only you knew, Cherry thought.

'One of the hardest things I found working

in hospitality was being able to stay calm in difficult situations in the kitchen, especially when I was under a temperamental chef. How do you think you would cope with that?'

Cherry paused, as she began to realise this was a sort of informal job interview.

Maybe. The first excitement began to surface but she forced it down. No one would want her for that sort of job. Anyway, she had no qualifications; she was here as a kitchen hand, in cold larder and food prep.

'I can stay calm. I've had lots of practice with that at home. I was the peacekeeper in our family.'

'Do you think you'd be interested in a traineeship?' Tam asked with a smile.

'As a kitchen hand?' Cherry was not going to get her hopes up.

'No, for a certificate three in commercial cookery. As we grow, we're going to need a lot more staff, and I like the idea of training the staff to suit our needs.'

'Oh my God, yes.' Cherry wanted to grab Tamsin and dance her along the path, but the last time she'd danced with excitement had not had a good outcome. 'Really? I was close once before but it fell through at the last minute. Just before I signed.' Her voice wavered; she still wouldn't let herself hope.

'Pippa was really impressed when she interviewed you. She's already applied for the traineeship funding, and once it's approved, we can formally offer you a traineeship. There's no one else under consideration. She was going to advertise, but we waited to see what you thought of the idea. Whether you're happy to stay for the long term.'

'Oh, wow.' Cherry fanned herself as expectation filtered in. 'That would be awesome. I'll do anything you need me to.' Now excitement was running though her like wildfire. Getting her trade qualification had been Cherry's dream since she'd stepped into her first restaurant, only to have it snatched away when sealing the deal was so close. 'Oh, Tam, thank you so much for having faith in me.'

'We're pretty confident we'll get the funding, but don't get too excited until we get the go ahead. But I'm sure we will. I just couldn't wait to see if you were interested. Sorry if I sprung it on you. Now I'll show you where your room is and wait for you to get changed. You'll be needed in the kitchen straight away.'

'I was a bit anxious about being late. I know you've got your function tonight.'

'It's okay. Jiminy called and let me know.

It's Race Week over on Hamo as I'm sure you know and he had to wait to get out of the marina. And don't stress, it's just an inhouse celebration. I'll talk to you more about the traineeship in the next few days. We've got a new chef on board now who'll make an excellent supervisor.'

Cherry tried to keep her voice calm. 'Having a qualification is something I've dreamed about ever since I started working in hospitality. I've tried a few times to get an apprenticeship in Brisbane and on the Gold Coast, but the competition down there is so fierce.' She pulled a face. 'Plus, I'm older than the applicants straight out of school.'

'Yeah. Most of them come out of school-based apprenticeships these days,' Tam said. 'Anyway—I'll show you your room and then I'll take you to meet Angus. If—when—it all gets approved, he'll be your supervisor. And the best part is, you'll be learning in a brand new kitchen.'

But Cherry had stopped listening.

Angus?

No, it couldn't be. She couldn't be that unlucky.

Could she?

Chapter Two

Angus

As soon as Pippa spoke, Angus Alexander put the knife down on the benchtop and took a step away; he was horrified by his unprofessional behaviour. 'I'm very sorry, Pippa.' His heart was thumping as he looked at Tamsin. 'And you too, Tamsin. Trust me, that will never happen again.'

He refused to look at Cherry, but he was aware that she'd stepped back into the corner of the kitchen. At least she'd stopped screeching at him. What made him even angrier was the burst of desire that had gripped him when she'd walked in. For a millisecond, he'd forgotten what a lying piece of work she was. His mouth had dropped open, and his heart had accelerated. He'd had to blink and look again, thinking it was wishful thinking and he'd conjured her up. Stupid thinking, but thoughts like that filled his head often.

But no, this time it was Cherry Chilcott in the flesh—looking as beautiful as ever—and he had to deal with it.

Angus knew that what he'd said, and his tone, were totally out of line. And maybe slightly exaggerated; incompetent and lazy had been a stretch, but as he'd dug for words they had been the first that had rolled off his tongue.

But, dishonest? No exaggeration there. Yes, Cherry Chilcott was certainly that. Could not be trusted as far as—

No, he refused to give any thought to her betrayal.

As for the knife in his hand, it had been unlucky that he'd been chopping vegetables when Tamsin had walked into the kitchen, with . . . with . . . *that* woman. He'd been so angry, he hadn't even realised the knife was in his hand when he'd pointed at her. The words had spewed out before he could think.

He would apologise to Pippa and Tamsin, but he would not apologise to Cherry Chilcott. She was the one who owed him an apology. She was the one who had wrecked his dream.

No apology. Even if it meant losing his job. *Not ever.*

He shut his mouth and jammed his lips together before he could dig a deeper hole for himself.

He wouldn't apologise, but he wasn't prepared to lose this job.

Pippa—the resort owner, and his employer—narrowed her eyes and looked from Cherry to him. 'Angus, I'd like a word now.

Privately, please.' Her voice was crisp and businesslike, and that made his behaviour seem even worse. She turned to Tamsin. 'Tam, show Cherry where everything is, and she can take over chopping the vegetables.'

'I have my knives in my bag.' Cherry said quietly as she slid the cloth bag off her shoulder.

Angus bit his tongue. One minute she'd been screaming like a banshee, now it was as though butter wouldn't melt in Cherry's mouth.

'And I can remember where most things are from when I worked here the night of the opening. I'll just wash up and get started,' she said.

Tamsin looked at Pippa, and Angus' stomach sank when they exchanged a look. So *she'd* worked here already, had she? They were going to take *her* side. He just knew it. Putting on the shy act had certainly got Cherry where she wanted to be.

Every time.

Poor little girl with no self-confidence. Bloody hell, her looks had blinded him and he'd fallen for the shy spiel, hook, line and sinker and then she'd reeled him in. The only thing he'd never been able to figure out was why she'd done it.

'Okay. I'll tell you what needs doing,' Tamsin said.

Angus swallowed and held back the

objection that threatened to spill out. He didn't want *Cherry* in his kitchen at all, let alone take over chopping his vegetables. He'd been stoked when he was offered the job on Pentecost Island, so he wasn't about to ruin his first week on duty by saying anything. The first two nights working with Tamsin had been great, and even though they were still in the old kitchen, they'd worked well together, and provided a three-course meal to twenty guests each night. Tamsin had been very receptive to his ideas and for the first time in his career as a chef, he was free to create his own menus.

Considering he was in charge tonight, and it was a special occasion, he knew his reaction had been totally unacceptable.

But, *shit*, Cherry Chilcott of all people.

They'd never had closure; that's why they'd both lost their cool. Angus took a deep breath; he couldn't believe he'd lost his temper so suddenly and so spectacularly. He wasn't one of those temperamental chefs, and he hated the thought that he'd come across that way to Tamsin and Pippa.

When Tamsin had brought Cherry into the kitchen, and she'd looked at him, and yelled, 'No way', he'd let fly straight back.

Pippa gestured to the door and he stood aside and let her lead the way. They turned towards the back of the house and he followed her onto the back lawn.

'I'm really sorry, Pippa,' he said again as she stopped beside the outdoor table. 'My behaviour was unac—'

'Sit down, Angus.'

He waited until Pippa was seated first and then he pulled out the wrought iron chair, sat down, and put his hands flat on the table. He was absolutely mortified that he had behaved like that, and worse, that Pippa and Tamsin had *both* witnessed his outburst.

'Okay, would you like to explain what that was all about?' Pippa leaned back and folded her arms as she stared at him.

Angus hesitated.

Pippa frowned and leaned forward. 'You used some very strong words to Cherry, and I'd like to know why. Is it personal, or do you have something you need to tell me with regard to her work?'

Again Angus hesitated as he desperately tried to think of what to say, and how to justify his outburst without looking like a fool, and possibly putting his new job in jeopardy.

'Oh, for goodness sake, Angus. We don't have all night. You have meals to prepare, and staff to supervise. Look, I thought I knew you, and I know Cherry—or at least I thought I did.' She lifted a hand and ran it over her hair. Her voice had calmed a fraction. 'I'm sure that behaviour was way out of character for both of you.'

He nodded.

'You called her incompetent, lazy and dishonest. Is there something I need to be aware of? Something that will interfere with the running of Ma Carmichael's?'

Angus froze. He opened his mouth and then he closed it. He needed to get his act together. Clearing his throat, he sat up straight and held Pippa's steady gaze.

'No. No there's not. I . . . um . . . exaggerated. She's not lazy or incompetent.' He held his hands together firmly on the table, so he wouldn't thump it. 'I'd like to say again I'm sorry for my outburst. I can reassure you that there is nothing I need to tell you. It was just a shock to see . . . her, and realise that she was working here tonight. It won't happen again.'

'Okay. Tell me about the dishonest bit? Do I need to worry about anything in terms of having her on staff here?'

'No.' He looked down. 'That was a personal matter.'

'So I guess, I'm not going to hear why you both behaved like that?'

Angus shook his head slowly. 'No. I can't

elaborate. I'm sorry. Even if it means my job is at stake.'

Pippa waved her hand impatiently. 'No, there are no jobs at stake. I just need a guarantee that the pair of you can work together without a repeat of that screaming match. I know what emotion can do, and I'm prepared to overlook this. Once. There's no room for personal issues in our resort. Can I have your word on that?'

'You have my word.' Angus nodded. 'Is she—' He couldn't even bring himself to say her name. It had taken him two years to stop thinking about her and what had happened. 'Is she just here for the night?'

'No. Cherry has already been hired, and I'm offering her a traineeship. You'll be her supervisor if she accepts. I'll speak to her too. Do I still have your word that you can work together?' Pippa stared at him, her gaze intent, and Angus bit back the dismay that jammed in his chest.

'Yes,' he repeated dully. 'You have my word.'

Bloody hell.

He would have to stick to it. Every other job he'd had since he'd trained had been in restaurants that were already established and he'd simply been one of the team that produced the meals. No flair, no creativity, no break to stretch himself so he could get the experience to start his own place up one day. He'd never had the chance to put his own mark on a restaurant, and now that Tamsin had offered him the opportunity to do that here, there was no way he was going to let the opportunity slide. He'd been dudded last time he was this close.

A brand new resort, a new restaurant with a state-of-the art-kitchen almost completed, and the chance to create his own menus and build his reputation; he had to stay. There was no decision to make.

Angus held back the groan that threatened and barely held on to his professionalism. Not only was *she* staying, he was supervising her.

But he'd be watching her, and the first step out of line, the first lie, and Cherry Chilcott would be gone.

He had no doubt that she'd stuff up; it was only a matter of waiting for when she did. She'd have an agenda, and she wouldn't be able to help herself.

***

When Pippa and Angus left the kitchen, Cherry let out the breath she'd been holding.

Tamsin threw her a glance. 'Those vegetables are for crudites to be served with a dip, so julienne them please. Do you know what that is?'

Cherry nodded. 'Yes. A matchstick cut.'

'Good.' Tamsin turned to leave, and Cherry felt dreadful. Her skin was prickling, and a mother of a headache was clawing at her temples. She pressed two fingers to her forehead hard, to ease the throbbing. She couldn't afford to get a migraine tonight. How could a day go downhill so quickly? One minute Tam had been telling her about an opportunity and now she was looking at her as though she'd crawled out from under a rock. When Tam had first mentioned Angus, she should have known. She should have turned around and run back to the wharf and called for Jiminy to take her away.

Damn, damn, damn.

'Tamsin, wait,' Cherry called out.

As Tamsin paused in the doorway, Mirabelle came back into the kitchen, her head down. There was a palpable tension in the kitchen that hadn't been there before.

'I'm sorry. That won't happen again,' Cherry said quietly. 'I hope I haven't stuffed up my chances of working here.'

Tamsin looked at her, but she didn't smile. 'Do you want to tell me what's going on?'

'I can't.' Cherry shook her head. 'It's not my story to tell.'

With a shrug Tamsin turned back to the door. 'I'll see what Pippa has to say.'

Without a word, Cherry reached into her bag to pull out her knife case. She couldn't ask for more than that.

Even though once she would have said he'd been the best thing to ever happen to her in her entire life, he had soon changed her mind. Closing her eyes, Cherry dragged in a deep breath wishing she'd never met Angus Alexander.

Never met him, and never fallen in love.

Chapter Three

Cherry - Two years earlier

The first time Cherry travelled overseas was a couple of weeks after her twenty-fifth birthday. Well, technically the trip was "over the sea", but because she didn't need a passport to get to Lord Howe Island, it probably couldn't be classed as international travel. Her siblings often teased Cherry about her stay-at-home attitude. Of course, Byron had done a year at Oxford University in the UK, and Leanne had been on a number of overseas sporting rep trips.

Cherry's trip to Lord Howe Island had been a spur of the moment decision. Her phone had rung when she was at work in the bar at Surfside on the Wednesday night when she was taking a break in the small staff room at the hotel.

'Hello?' Cherry tucked her phone between her shoulder and cheek as she filled the kettle. The sandwich she'd brought to work was toasting under the grill.

'I'd like to speak to Cherry please.'

'Mum, it's me,' she said.

'Oh, it didn't sound like you. Where are you?'

'I'm at work.'

'But where's that? I forget where you're working now.'

Cherry resisted the eye roll that threatened. 'I'm still at Surfside down on the coast. I've been here for a year now, Mum.'

'Oh. I thought you were going to look for a real job. Anyway, no matter. We want you to come home for the weekend.'

Surprise filled her. 'For my birthday?'

'Um, yes. And for Leanne's news.' Her mother's voice held a tinge of apology, but no matter how much Mum understood the family situation, she'd never once stood up for Cherry.

Maybe that's where my own lack of self-confidence comes from, she thought.

'Byron will be home from Sydney for the weekend, and Leanne said she'll stay on Saturday night. Please come home, sweetheart. It'll be like old times.'

Great, can't wait.

'I'm not sure if I'm working that weekend, Mum,' Cherry lied with her fingers crossed. She knew she had this weekend off.

'It's ages since we've all been together. The time just goes too fast, doesn't it? And Leanne is so excited.'

'Mmm,' Cherry said as she opened the grill

and slid a plate beneath her toastie. 'It just does.'

'Anyway, Leanne has news and she wants us all to be together when she tells us she's getting married.'

'Don't we already know?' Cherry carefully cut the crusty edges from her sandwich.

'Yes, but this is the official telling,' Mum said. 'You could make a cake. For your birthday. It would save me thinking of a dessert after dinner.'

'Okay, I'll text you if I can get time off work. If I come I'll bring a cake. Bye, Mum.'

Tess, one of her work colleagues was sitting at the table and looked up at Cherry sympathetically when she disconnected the call. 'A summons home?

Cherry pulled a face. 'Yes.'

'My mum's given up,' Tess said. 'Every time I went home I'd end up in an argument with my two brothers and their wives. They think working in a bar is not a job for a woman.'

'Yeah, I know.' Cherry pulled out the chair and sat opposite Tess. 'Mum thinks I'm a waitress. Dad would demand I came home if he knew I was working in the bar.' She shook her head ruefully. 'Even though I'm twenty-five.'

'Families, hey?' Tess said.

In the end Cherry gave in—as she always did—and found herself sitting at the family dinner table on Saturday night, wishing she was a million miles away.

'I'm very pleased you're getting married, Leanne.' Dad said. 'You'll be a very beautiful bride. Who are you going to have as your bridesmaids?'

Leanne sighed. 'I don't know, Daddy. It's so hard to choose. All my friends have been ringing up and begging me to ask them because they know it's going to be the wedding of the year.'

'Don't ask me, don't ask me,' Cherry prayed silently. Although she knew there'd be no chance of that.

'It's so hard when I've got so many close girlfriends. I don't know who to pick as my chief bridesmaid. They all want to be that.' Leanne shot a sly glance at her little sister, but Cherry ignored her.

If you think I'm going to be upset, you don't know me at all.

She zoned out for the next ten minutes as the possibility of the local golf club was mooted by Dad as the reception venue, and Mum moved the conversation on to menus and flowers.

Gah, kill me now, Cherry thought as the colour of dresses and the need to get perfectly matching roses was discussed. Sometimes she wished she could say and do what she was thinking. At that moment, she was thinking of putting her finger down her throat and gagging.

Finally, Dad turned to Byron who was looking as though he'd zoned out too. 'And Byron, your new job at the university sounds just the ticket.'

'It is, Dad. I've been offered a great research topic.'

Dad beamed.

Mum shot Cherry a glance. 'Would you like a piece of cake, Randall? Cherry made it for her birthday.'

'No, it looks too sickly sweet for me.' Her father stared across the table. 'So another birthday? How old now? Twenty-seven? Time you had a decent job, girl.'

'No, I'm only twenty-five, Dad,' Cherry said quietly.

'Well, it's past time you did something with your life. Took a leaf out of your brother and sister's book. A couple of my friends from golf have got local businesses. I might be able to put a word in for you this week. Can you type?'

'I won't be here.' Cherry stared at her father wondering—hoping—if there was any chance she'd been adopted.

His brows were in need of a trim, the white tufts contrasting with the black hair she was sure Dad dyed. He'd dripped gravy onto his white golf shirt, and there was a smear of mashed potato on his upper lip.

Cherry bit back a laugh.

A real charmer. Maybe Mum had an affair and I am a love child. That would explain why I'm such a misfit in the family. Why my father hates me so much.

Her father raised those eyebrows and Cherry stared fascinated as one long white hair curled across the top of his nose. 'Where will you be?'

'I'll be out of touch for a while.'

'Where are you going, sis?' Byron asked. He was okay; her brother's focus was always in a different world, but he was never nasty to Cherry.

Leanne was a totally different matter; her problem with Cherry had started when they were teenagers. One of Mum's sisters had been overheard talking to Mum. 'Byron and Leanne might be the high achievers,' Aunty Jenny had said, 'but Cherry is the good looking one of your three, Narelle.' Leanne had never forgotten that, and now, even ten years later, she went out of her way to make Cherry feel inadequate.

And succeeded.

Cherry bit her lip as Byron waited for her answer; she tried to think of somewhere where she could say she was having a holiday. Her gaze settled on the placemat underneath the fruit bowl on the kitchen benchtop. The placemat that Mum had brought home from their honeymoon, over thirty years before.

'Lord Howe Island,' she said quietly. 'It's a place I've always wanted to visit. You've often said how beautiful it is.'

Surprisingly that got a positive response from Dad. 'It's a great place. Your mother and I always meant to go back.'

'We will one day,' Mum said.

'Who are you going with, Chezza?' Leanne said in a super-sweet tone.

'No one,' she replied. 'I'm having a holiday by myself.'

'Boring.' Leanne rolled her eyes. 'Still Nellie-No-Friends?'

'It's not a boring place, Leanne,' Dad snapped.

'I'm happy with my own company.' Cherry tried not to smile; Leanne copping Dad's criticism was a rare occurrence. 'I'm looking forward to it. You'll have to tell me the best places to go when I'm there, Dad.'

'You have to feed the fish at Ned's Beach,' Dad said. The conversation that followed was actually pleasant as her parents told her about snorkelling and the walks on the island.

Leanne pulled out her phone and ignored them.

On Cherry's way back to the coast, the idea had taken root, and she decided to take the leave that was owed to her, and actually have a holiday.

Three days later, the date was set, the air tickets bought, and her accommodation at a small lodge was booked.

The fact that she was taking a trip by herself, and that her sister found it unfathomable, didn't bother her. She'd learned at an early age that her family didn't understand her, or particularly care about her.

If your own family let you down, what hope did she have of making friends with anyone? Tess was about the closest person she had as a friend, and they'd only had coffee a few times in the year that Tess had worked there. Besides, Cherry was used to her own company; she had no need of anyone.

Chapter Four

Angus-two years earlier

'Mate, it's the most boring place on earth.' Angus' golfing mate, Craig Roberts, lifted his beer and finished it in one gulp. He wiped the back of his hand over his mouth and shook his head. 'You can see the island in a day, the guests are in their eighties, and if the weather blows up, you could get stuck there for weeks.'

Angus raised his eyebrows. 'Sounds like a different place to what I've heard. My sister's partner was a teacher out there, and lived on the island for two years. Said he loved the place.'

'Was he a fisherman?'

Angus nodded. 'Yeah, Brad's a fishing tragic. They're in Cairns now.'

'What about you? Do you fish?'

'No, but I know how to cook it. Anyway, I've been offered a job at one of the resorts there, so I'm going to go over and take a look before I even think about it.' Angus put his glass down. 'Not that cooking fish is my thing.'

'I know,' Craig said with a nod. 'You're going to get that fancy beef from your family's farm and open up a chain of steakhouses. What were they going to be called? AA's? From paddock to plate?'

'God, you love taking the piss, don't you?' Angus picked up his keys. 'If I didn't feel sorry for you you'd have no one to drink with, Robbo.'

'Mate, I've got more friends than you've had hot breakfasts.'

'AA's is going to be a top-class one-off restaurant one day, you wait and see.' Angus slid off the bar stool. 'Gotta go, mate. Speaking of hot breakfasts, I've got a breakfast shift in the morning.' He looked at his friend curiously. 'I didn't know you'd been to Lord Howe Island?'

'I haven't.' Craig shook his head and chuckled. 'Mate, you'd go batshit crazy living on any island.'

Angus laughed. 'So you're an expert. I'll go and check it out. You could always come with me.'

'No way, mate. I'm heading up to Cairns in a couple of weeks. Now that's where you should look for a job. Change your plans and come with me.'

'Too late. I'm booked for Friday.'

'Okay, I'll catch you for a beer when you get back and I can say I told you so.'

'I'll send you a postcard,' Angus called over his shoulder as his mate followed him out of the pub.

'Don't bother.' Craig walked over to his

SUV and chuckled. 'See you when you get back. Unless you get stuck there.'

##

Three days later as the sun was about to peek over the horizon, Angus parked his car in the long-term parking station at Brisbane airport. The weather was clear and still, and he hoped it was like that on the island. Even though he was going there to suss out the restaurant, he was looking forward to taking a break. Work had been hectic lately, but it was the lack of variety in his job that was boring him. When he'd got his qualification, Angus had had a dream, but now he seemed to be going backwards in his current place of work. At each restaurant when he'd accepted the positions, promises had been made, but he'd always ended up doing the mundane work.

His father would have been the first to criticise.

He'd come home to the huge family property in the Gulf of Carpentaria after his final year at boarding school. 'Cooking in restaurants! A bloody waste of time. You don't want to do the cattle work? You want to cook? You can stay here and be the camp cook for the musters.'

Being someone who always did the right

thing, Angus followed his father's wish and stayed on the property, even though he'd hated every minute of what he was doing. Out in the paddocks, helping to muster, pulling wire for the never-ending fencing, he swallowed his resistance and pitched in and helped. As he worked, he had dreamed of a different life.

Angus had discovered his love for creating food in year ten. Cooking had helped him forget how much he dreaded going home, knowing it was expected he would spend his life on the isolated property. Cooking made him feel good about himself when he saw the pleasure that the students and staff got out of trying recipes that he created for his course. In his final year, he'd done a school-based traineeship and worked in a city restaurant in Brisbane two days a week. He'd loved every second of it and was sure they would offer him an apprenticeship when one came up, but it hadn't ensued—or so he'd thought.

A chance comment from his mother a few months after he moved home changed Angus' life.

'I know you're not happy here, love, but your father thought it was best for him to say no to the job. You'll grow to love it here and this spread will be all yours one day.'

Angus put his muddy boots on the veranda and looked up at his mother as she held the screen door open. His brow wrinkled in a frown as he stared at her.

'Say no to what job?'

Mum had looked away as her hand went to her mouth.

'Mum? What did you mean?'

'I thought you knew,' she said softly. 'Dad said he was going to tell you. I thought you'd accepted it was for the best and got on with the real work.'

Angus had struggled to keep his voice calm, as anger burned in his chest. 'Tell me exactly what you're referring to. Please.'

She wouldn't meet his eye. 'That restaurant in Brisbane that you worked at when you were at school last year, they called here when you were away on your schoolies' trip with your friends.'

'Keep going.'

'They wanted to talk to you, but Dad talked to them instead. They were going to offer you a full apprenticeship, but Dad said you wouldn't be taking it as you had to work on the property.'

Disappointment vied with anger as Angus stared at his gentle mother. The smidgeon of respect that he still held for his father disappeared in an instant.

'No, he never told me.' He turned sad eyes to Mum. 'And that was essentially a lie, wasn't it?

If you can't trust your own flesh and blood to want the best for you and tell the truth, who can you trust?'

It only took him an hour to pack what he wanted to take with him, and he was gone before his father came in that night.

Even Mum's tears as he loaded up his old ute, and as she clung to him when he said goodbye, didn't break his resolve.

The restaurant in Brisbane had of course moved on to someone else, and what stuck in Angus' throat was the fact that it had to be one of the guys in the course he hadn't got on with. Alan Garner was the type who used other people to make himself look good. Stealing ideas, passing them off as his own. He and Angus had come head to head a number of times. He was one of Craig's golf buddies, so Angus had given away golf in the past few months too.

Angus had started work in a small restaurant that was part of a chain, and put himself through the course.

No, there was no way he was going to fail and fulfill his father's expectations. By the time he was thirty, Angus intended having his own restaurant. He had three years to get there, and the rate at which time was running out spurred him on.

Angus shoved his thoughts aside as he

grabbed his single bag from the back of the SUV before making his way to the domestic terminal to catch the early flight to Sydney. He hated waiting around, and he'd picked a flight that landed in Sydney thirty minutes before he was due to board the Lord Howe flight. He glanced at his watch as he crossed into the terminal; no luggage to check in, so there'd be time for coffee.

As much as he knew Robbo had been joking, Angus wondered whether there was an element of truth beneath his words. Maybe a small island wasn't the place to get the experience he was after. Since he'd finished his training three years ago, Angus had worked in four different restaurants, and had left each of them, disillusioned. *The Happy Cow* where he worked now —what a stupid name for a restaurant—was turning out much the same. The experience that had been promised at each establishment had never eventuated. He felt as though he was being used and that his career was stalling before it had even really started.

Crossing the wide concourse, he joined the early breakfast queue at the coffee shop, and mulled over his problem. Maybe the restaurant on Lord Howe Island would be right for him, and give him the chance to develop his career. At the rate he was going, he might as well work in a pub bistro and serve up steaks, and fish and chips every night.

When he got to the island, he was not going to let on he was a chef; he'd check out the restaurant anonymously. Then if Trader Bob's, the one where he'd been offered a sous chef position, suited his needs, he'd think about it.

He wasn't going to rush into a job again. The last time he'd done that he'd landed at the bloody *Happy Cow*.

He smiled at the girl who served him as she tried to talk him into a big breakfast. 'A big strapping guy like you needs more than you'll get on the plane,' she said with a wink.

'No, thanks, just a flat white.'

That pre-prepared food wrapped in paper under the glass counter wasn't real food. She fluttered her eyelashes at him as she gestured to the container beside the cash register. 'A muffin then?'

He shook his head. 'No, thanks.'

With a shrug she turned to the coffee machine and soon the sound of frothing milk killed any conversation.

She passed the coffee to Angus, took his payment and turned to the next customer. 'A big breakfast, sir?'

Angus smiled as he carried his coffee to the boarding gate. He sat and sipped his coffee as he watched the crowds go by. At this time of the morning, it was predominantly made up of men and women in business suits, all looking very serious and each intent on their phones or laptops.

As he watched, his gaze narrowed when a beautiful woman walked across and stood at the coffee counter. Her white jeans and olive-green T-shirt stood out like a beacon in the sea of black.

After she took her coffee from the same girl who had served him, the woman turned and moved gracefully through the crowd. Tall and slim, with raven black hair that reached almost to her waist, her gaze stayed down as she crossed the boarding lounge and took a seat opposite him. A faint whiff of something sweet lingered after she walked past his seat, sat down and finally lifted her head. She gave him a cursory glance as her eyes swept the terminal before she pulled a small reading device from her bag and turned her attention to that.

Although her olive-green eyes matched the rest of her—vivid and beautiful—they seemed to hold a shyness as she looked past him and then quickly lowered her head without making eye contact.

Angus found it hard to look away, but his neck warmed with embarrassment when he realised he was staring. He pulled out his phone and browsed the news. In the fifteen minutes before the flight was called, his gaze was drawn back to her several times, but not once did she look up or move as she read.

'Flight SN 512 now boarding at Gate Thirty.'

Angus waited for a moment to allow her to stand first, but when the woman didn't look up from her reading, he assumed she was catching another flight. He stood, swung his bag over his shoulder and headed for the gate.

Chapter Five

Cherry - two years earlier

Cherry had been well aware of the attention of the guy opposite her in the boarding lounge, but she chose to ignore it. No matter how hard she tried to blend into a crowd, no matter how much she dressed down, she always seemed to catch someone's attention. Today she had worn a pair of jeans and a plain green T-shirt, left off the chunky wooden beads she loved, and wore nothing really fashionable, but the guy opposite kept looking up from his phone, and staring at her. Maybe he'd recognised her from the bar at Surfside?

When the flight was called, she knew he was waiting for her to go first. He put his phone away and sat straight, but she kept reading. Finally after he got up and disappeared through the gate, she picked up her bag and followed. The flight was only half-full and she paid no attention to anyone after she handed her boarding pass to the attendant, and settled in her seat near the front.

As her attention left the story she'd been immersed in, Cherry's flying phobia kicked in fast, and she was already regretting her rash decision to take this spur of the moment holiday. She reached up and opened the vent above her and let the cool breeze play on her hot face. Her hands were clammy and she flexed her fingers slowly to let the cool air flow between them. Her skin burned and tension began to build across the base of her neck as the attendants began the safety briefing. She'd told herself all week that she was no longer scared of flying. But then foolishly she'd watched a show about air disasters two nights ago, and her trepidation had come slamming back.

Just think about how many planes are in the air every day. Every *hour*. And Australia had the best safety record in the world. Her breathing eased a little and then there was a whir and a clunk from outside the plane and her mouth dried.

We are still on the ground, she told herself firmly.

If there had been a way to get off the plane, Cherry would have taken it. She closed her eyes, grateful that there was no one sitting beside her. A moment later she jumped when a gentle hand touched her shoulder.

'Please put your window blind up, madam,' the attendant said with a smile.

Cherry nodded and with shaking hands lifted the blind. How the hell was she going to fly across the ocean for two hours to Lord Howe Island when she boarded the next flight?

To Cherry's surprise and extreme relief, she survived the flight to Sydney without the plane crashing, or her descending into full screaming panic mode.

One down. One to go, she thought as she stood on the escalator that took her up to the departure lounge for the next flight.

No, one down, three to go. I have to get home again.

Her stomach was churning—maybe nerves, maybe hunger—but she wasn't game to eat anything until she was on the ground on the island. After a quick detour to the bathroom, she sat in the small departure lounge and pulled out her Kindle. At least the book had her attention, and she could focus on that.

As she sat there reading, the back of her chair dipped slightly as someone sat behind her. A woodsy aftershave aroma tickled her nose, but she didn't turn.

After a few moments, a voice came over the PA system. 'Passengers heading for Lord Howe Island on Flight ST2254 please be advised that your flight has been delayed due to adverse weather conditions. We apologise for any inconvenience. We should have you boarding within the next two hours, but we will keep you informed.'

'At least it's not a problem with the plane,' a deep voice said behind her.

When no one replied, Cherry realised that the comment had been directed at her, and she sat forward and turned around.

Her gaze encountered a pair of warm brown eyes and a smile. She nodded. 'That's something, I suppose.'

It was the nice-looking guy who'd been staring at her at Brisbane airport, and her heart kicked up a notch.

'Do I know you?' she asked quietly. 'I mean, I'm sorry, I noticed you looking at me in Brisbane and I wondered if we'd met and I'd forgotten.'

Her cheeks heated with embarrassment. That had sounded like a pickup line.

'No. No, I'm sorry. You probably thought I was being stalkerish, but if I'm going to be honest I was going to say I was looking at you because of how pretty you are, and what an unusual colour your eyes are.' He smacked his hand to his forehead. 'I'm sorry, that sounded like a standard pickup line, didn't it?'

Cherry dropped her gaze as shyness flooded through her, but she smiled. 'No. I was just thinking that what I said sounded like one. It's fine.'

'So I guess we're in for a bit of a wait,' he said. 'That is, if you're going to Lord Howe Island.'

His deep voice and gentle tone were soothing, and Cherry relaxed a little. She turned her Kindle off and slipped it into her bag.

'I think I am, although the flight delay is not what I needed.'

'You *think* you are?' He tipped his head to the side and a shock of brown curls fell over his forehead. The way his hand automatically lifted and pushed them back looked like a well-practised move.

Cherry shrugged. 'I booked my flights close so there wasn't long to wait, because I knew I'd be nervous, and would probably chicken out. This delay makes it more likely.'

'The small planes are better than the jets,' he said.

'Small planes? What do you mean small planes?' Her heart rose into her throat.

He must have thought she was joking because he chuckled. 'Not that small, but it's always more reassuring for me to hear propellers than the whine of a jet engine.'

Cherry widened her eyes. 'Just how small is this plane? It's going over the sea. A long way!' She couldn't help the rise in pitch of her voice.

'It's a Dash 8. Not too small. A thirty-six

seater. And they have the best safety record. The
only Dash 8 crashes have been due to pilot error,
and I know for a fact that there's only a handful of
pilots who are allowed to land at Lord Howe
because of the cross winds and the short runway.
It's not long enough for the big planes or
inexperienced pilots. So we're in excellent hands.
And we'll have a safe trip and be there before you
know it.'

Cherry raised a shaking hand to her mouth
and the guy frowned.

'You're not joking. You really are nervous,
aren't you? I'm sorry if I frightened you.'

'I am.' She nodded and put her hand down.
'Maybe I'll just go and catch a train back to
Brisbane.'

'Would you think I was being forward if I
suggested having a coffee together? Just to keep
your mind occupied while we wait. It would be a
shame to miss out on your holiday because you
were nervous about a short—and very safe—
flight.'

Normally Cherry's shyness would have
meant a refusal, but there was something about this
guy that made her feel at ease. 'Okay. Thank you.'

He stood and came around to her side of the
back-to-back seats. Cherry was tall, but when she
stood he towered over her.

'Angus Alexander. I'm pleased to meet you.' He held out his hand.

Cherry took his hand and her fingers were held in a gentle grasp. 'Cherry Chilcott and likewise.'

The coffee shop was only a short distance from the boarding gate, and Angus pulled out a chair from a table close to the concourse. 'So we can hear any announcements and keep an eye on the departures board.'

'Sounds like a plan.'

'My shout. What sort of coffee?' he asked.

'Caramel latte, please.'

'Coming right up.' His warm—and constant—smile relaxed her even more.

Cherry sat back and looked around the terminal as she waited. It was deliberate, because as much as she didn't want to be obvious, her gaze was drawn to Angus. She liked the way he spoke, the way he moved and how thoughtful he was. It was really unusual for her to be this relaxed in a guy's company so quickly. Not that she hadn't dated since she'd moved to the Gold Coast; she had, and for a brief, stupid three weeks about five years ago she'd tried living with a guy.

And hadn't mentione*d that* when she went home.

She should have known better; the

relationship had died a natural death—"because you're boring, Cherry,"—and she knew that she was happier alone. The breakup hadn't hurt, but her low self-confidence had taken a beating.

Again.

Since then, she'd gone out a few times with a group from work, and the occasional coffee with Tess, but always kept herself aloof.

Finally she allowed her gaze to wander to the counter where Angus was waiting to order their coffee. He was tall, and Cherry's stomach fluttered as her eyes travelled down from broad shoulders, a torso tapering to a narrow waist, and then lower to denims that hugged strong thighs. Forcing her gaze back to the holiday crowd milling in the airport— very different to the morning crowd in Brisbane— she wondered why a guy like that would be travelling alone. Maybe he lived on the island and had a partner there; he seemed to know a lot about the planes and the pilots that flew this route. Maybe he flew back and forth often.

Maybe there was a wife and kids waiting for him on the island.

She jumped when a tray slid onto the table, and a tantalising aroma of coffee and something baked wafted up towards her.

'I was starving so I bought us one each,' he said. She flicked a glance at his left hand and hid a smile when there was no ring. 'I hope you like friands? They've warmed them up. Raspberry and white chocolate.'

'Yum, I do. Thank you.'

Angus sat down and passed her coffee over. 'Sugar?'

'No, thanks. The caramel is sweet enough.' She looked at him from beneath her lashes. 'Not to mention raspberry and white chocolate.'

There was silence for a while as they both sipped their coffee.

'So tell me, a holiday or work?' Angus broke the quiet just as Cherry felt it was getting uncomfortable.

She put her cup down. 'Just a short holiday. How about you? I wondered if you lived on the island.'

His laugh was deep. 'Me? No. I'm a farm boy from North Queensland. I've never been to an island before.'

'So a holiday for you too?'

He paused for a moment before nodding. 'Yes, a holiday.'

'There seems to be a lot to do on the island. For such a small place, that is,' she added. 'My parents went there for their honeymoon and they loved it.'

'I haven't had much of a chance to see

what's on offer. Just a quick read of the brochure. What appealed to you?'

Cherry tipped her head to the side and put one finger on her lips. 'There's all the touristy stuff. Fish feeding, snorkelling, fishing, golf, a few restaurants, but the thought of doing lots of walking appeals to me.' She looked away from him. 'I'm not really one for organised activities.'

'Nor me,' he said. 'And I'm certainly not a fisherman.'

She wondered why he smiled again.

'What appealed to me most is that it's got a cap on the number of visitors allowed,' Cherry added.

'That might explain why there's only a few restaurants on the island,' he said. 'Where are you staying?'

'In one of the lodges between the beach and the lagoon.' Cherry felt comfortable telling him.

'Me too. The travel agent said they were centrally located. I was surprised there's no car hire. Only bicycles.'

Cherry pulled a face. 'I know. I can't ride one.'

'Really? You'll have to learn while you're there. How come you can't?'

She shrugged. 'I never had one when I was a child. We lived on a busy road and my mum was always worried we'd get run over.'

'We?'

'Yes, me and a brother and a sister. What about you?'

'One sister, so I'm the only son. And that puts the pressure on.' Angus lifted his coffee and sipped, but didn't elaborate.

He finished his coffee before they spoke again and there were only crumbs left of his friand. He pointed to hers. 'Eat up, or it'll get cold.'

As Cherry picked up her plastic fork and pushed the cake around the plate, a call came over the PA.

'Passengers travelling to Lord Howe Island on ST2254, please make your way to the boarding gate. The weather has cleared and boarding has been brought forward; the flight will depart in fifteen minutes.'

'Oh, I didn't even have time to get nervous,' she said.

Angus stood and waited for her. 'What seat are you in?'

Cherry took out her boarding pass, and looked at it. 'Row 2F.'

'A happy coincidence.' His smile lit up his face. 'I hope you're not sick of my company, because I'm in 2E.'

A pleasurable tingle shot through Cherry

and she smiled. 'I think I can put up with your company for a while longer.' She tipped her head to the side and frowned, before she gave into her worry. 'It's only a two-hour flight, isn't it?'

He nodded solemnly. 'It is, and if you get sick of my chatter, you can always read your book.'

Chapter Six

Pentecost Island-Pippa

I looked across the table at Tamsin and I could see she was still on edge from the ruckus in the kitchen. I nudged her foot under the table and caught her eye. 'Relax,' I mouthed quietly when she looked across the table at me.

Rafe and Gabe were deep in conversation, arguing about the upcoming football season. Rafe was shaking his head.

'Football is a *round* ball. The rest of those Aussie games are just pale imitations.'

Gabe looked at him with a grin. 'Mate, if you're going to marry an Aussie, you have to learn that real football is *not* soccer. It's rugby league.'

Tam leaned forward and spoke quietly to me. Rafe and I were sitting at the narrow middle section of the U next to Evie and Jed; Gabe and Tam were on our right. We'd not said anything to the others about the situation that we'd left behind in the kitchen.

'I can't relax,' she said quietly. 'Who knows if we'll even get a meal. Do you know how hard it was to leave them in *my* kitchen?'

'They both gave me their word that they'd behave.' I stared over her head to the path that led to the house and nodded. 'And they must have done that because here comes Mirabelle with the entrees now.'

Tamsin put one hand to her chest. 'Thank goodness for that. I was terrified your night was going to be ruined. It was me who gave them both the jobs.'

'Uh uh.' I shook my head. 'I interviewed Cherry.'

'Yeah, but I said how good she was. She was when I worked with her.'

'Well, they've obviously got a history of some sort together. A personal one.'

'Who's that, love?' Rafe's warm breath brushed my cheek. 'You both look very serious. You're supposed to be having a good time. It's our pre-wedding party.'

'Ha,' I said. 'And who's talking about football?'

'Sorry. It won't happen again, will it, Gabe?'

'Not at all,' Gabe replied with an innocent smile as he put his arm around Tam. 'You okay?' he asked.

'Yeah, just a kitchen problem, but hey, I'm not working tonight so they—it can sort itself out.' Tam caught my eye and we giggled.

'What's so funny?' Nell asked from the

other side of the table. She and Nat were sitting beside Eliza and Phillippe, and Sienna was beside Eliza.

'Just a little television type drama with some temperamental kitchen staff. All good.'

Tamsin and I composed ourselves and I waited for Mirabelle to put the platter at our end of the table. I touched her arm as she pulled back. 'All good in the kitchen?' I asked quietly.

She nodded. 'There's been no bloodshed and the talk is extremely polite.' As she turned away, she whispered. 'Although you could cut the air with a knife.'

Tam rolled her eyes. 'Don't mention knives.'

'What's going on, ladies?' Rafe persisted.

'I'll tell you later. The entrée's getting cold.'

##

The situation in the kitchen was obviously under control because by the time the dessert came out we had been served an excellent meal, and there had been a constant supply of hot and cold finger food to the bar. Eliza's idea of charging for an all-inclusive Saturday night package of all you can eat plus a bottle of wine, or six beers, was working well. Nat had ensured that the drinks flowed, both to our table and to the yachties who now moved to a table near the beach. Tamsin and I had relaxed.

Rafe stood as Mirabelle finished clearing the dessert plates away, and tapped a teaspoon on the side of his wine glass.

'Can I have your attention please, ladies and gentlemen.' My famous English author fiancé spoke in his poshest voice. No matter what he said, Rafe's voice still sent a warm shiver down my spine.

He turned with a grin as I tugged at his sleeve. 'No speeches, Rafe.'

'Yeah, save that for the wedding,' Tamsin chimed in.

'I want to speak,' he said. A thrill shot through me as he placed his hand on my shoulder and I looked up at him. I still found it hard to believe that I was going to marry this man in two weeks. We'd come a long way since we'd argued over possession of the land on Pentecost Island, and had ended up spending a night up a tree together when Rafe had rescued me from a feral goat.

The smiles around the table, the happy voices and the company of our closest friends filled me with joy and drew me back to the present. Rafe had been a big part of bringing me to this state of perpetual happiness, but a great deal of credit had to go to my friends—both new and old. We girls were a tight group, and we all looked out for each other.

Evie would be missed, but I knew the dynamic would change as more staff moved to the island, and we got busier as the resort grew.

'Just a quick word that I'm sure you'll all agree with. Please lift your glasses and toast our long-wed-newlywed couple over there.' He lifted his glass. 'To Jed and Evie. Wishing you a lifetime of happiness.'

We all stood and lifted our glasses. 'To Jed and Evie.'

When we were all seated again Evie put her hand on Jed's shoulder and stood. 'I'd like to say a few words too.' Her cheeks were flushed pink, and as she looked around the group, her smile was full of joy. 'I want to say thank you for the wonderful months I spent working on the island. As much as I'm going to love being with Jed'—her husband reached up and squeezed her hand—'I'm going to miss you all—*and* my gardens and forest glades very much.'

'It's not going to be the same without you here,' Sienna called out.

'I've never had many friends in my life,' Evie continued, 'but you all welcomed me with open arms and you made me feel as though I belonged. So I want to propose a toast.' Her eyes were full of laughter as Jed passed Evie's glass up to her. 'All for one and—'

'And one for all,' the rest of the women at the table chorused.

Once the laughter had stopped, Evie remained standing. 'I have one more thing to say. Jed and I have some big news. We're moving north. He's going to move his business to Mackay, and we'll put *Kestrel* in the marina there.'

Chapter Seven

Angus-Two years earlier

The propellers began to spin, and the two flight stewards buckled themselves into the seats facing the passengers. Angus had become aware of Cherry's tension building as the crew had gone through the flight briefing. Her hands were clenched on her lap, and she jiggled her feet on the floor nervously. Once the plane began to taxi out to the runway, she lifted one hand and pushed back a strand of raven black hair and looked across at him. He guessed the tight grimace that twisted her pretty lips was supposed to be a smile.

'Would you like a drink as soon as we're in the air?' he asked. 'It might help calm you.'

'I'm okay,' she said. 'Once we get off the ground I like looking down at the houses. It's like a little fairy-tale land, isn't it?'

Angus nodded noncommittally. He had a feeling that the plane would take off into the wind—the east—and that there would only be blue ocean beneath them until they reached Lord Howe Island. Not little fairyland houses. 'Tell me a little bit more about the island,' he said. 'I didn't get any time to read up on it in detail.'

'Didn't you?' her eyes were wide, but she seemed a little bit less nervous. 'Didn't you plan your holiday?'

'No. I was too busy at work,' he said.

'What sort of work do you do?' she asked.

He grinned at her. 'You tell me. What do you think I do?' He tried to distract her; it was easy to see tell she was terrified about the take off. For a moment he considered taking her hand, but decided that was a bit too forward.

Cherry tipped her head to the side and he noticed her hand was shaking as she raised one finger to her lips. 'An engineer,' she said so softly he had to bend his head to hear her voice over the engines. Close enough, he got another whiff of her perfume and moved back.

'Nope. But I'm intrigued. What made you say that?'

'Because you knew so much about the plane, and the flight and the pilot and the runway on the island.' Her voice was a little firmer now. 'How did you know all that?'

'Because my sister used to live out on the island and she told me. Her partner was the teacher at the school. I'll be in her bad books when she hears I went out there. She was always trying to get me to visit when they lived there. Okay, so guess again.'

This time her lips lifted in a proper smile. 'There's a lot of careers to choose from.'

'Okay, so keep guessing.' The note of the engines changed as she looked at him, but Cherry didn't appear to notice.

'A teacher? Same reasons. You know so much stuff.'

'No,' he said with a chuckle. 'I wasn't a good student. I went to boarding school in Brisbane. I hated school, but I loved being away from the isolation of the property.'

'Can I give up now?'

Angus' gaze slid to the window beside her. They were about to take off and, as he watched, the plane lifted and a few seconds later there was a thump as the wheels came up. He turned back to see an olive-green gaze fixed on him intently.

'Well? Can I give up?' she repeated.

'No way.' He shook his head. 'We have a two-hour trip to get through.'

'A psychologist?'

'No.'

'A doctor?'

'Hell no. You have to be smart for that.'

'Well, I'm going to give—' Before Cherry could finish her sentence. the plane hit an air pocket, dropped a metre or so, and shuddered a bit to one side. Her head swivelled quickly to the window and she looked down and gasped. 'Oh my God, we're off the ground, we're above the water.' Her face blanched and she gripped the arms of the seat. Her eyes were wide with fright.

Before he could think, Angus reached out and took her small soft hands between his. 'Take a deep breath and look at me, Cherry.'

She stared at his hands for a moment before lifting her eyes to him. 'I'm sorry. I'm being silly. I'm okay.'

Her eyes were still intent on his and he took the opportunity to look back at her. Really look at her. There was a tiny freckle near the hairline above her forehead and a small faded white scar above her right eyebrow. Apart from those two tiny imperfections there was not a mark on Cherry's skin.

Unless you counted the pink flush that deepened high on her beautiful cheekbones as she looked back at him.

'That's what good seat buddies are for. To reassure you.' As he stared at her, being a casual seat buddy was a long way from his thoughts. The jolt that had hit him square in the chest as the tip of her tongue came out and moistened her lips had nothing to do with being an impartial seat buddy.

Angus swallowed and looked along the aisle as the whir of trolley wheels reached him. 'Look, they're about to serve lunch. How about a wine to go with it?'

Cherry swallowed. 'Um, isn't it a bit early?

He flashed a wide smile at her, trying to hide the intensity of the feeling that was rocketing through him. Nothing like that had ever happened to him before. 'Nothing's too early when you're on holidays, is it?'

The flight attendant stopped beside their seat and Angus finally let go of Cherry's hands.

'I'm guessing white?' he said.

This time it was Cherry who grinned. 'You're guessing wrong.'

Angus raised his eyebrows. 'You're a red drinker?'

'I am, but it still feels a bit early in the day.'

'I have a light rosé, madam.' The steward had followed their conversation with interest.

'Then that would be perfect,' Cherry said.

'I'll join you. Make that two, please.' Angus tried not to flinch when the two packets of airline nibbles were placed on their trays next to the plastic cups holding their wine. He picked one up, examined the contents and put it back down.

'Not hungry?' Cherry asked as she sipped at her drink.

'No, I'll wait until we land.' Angus glanced at his watch. 'And that is only one hour and forty seven minutes away, so you have a while left to guess my profession.'

The cheeky grin that lifted those pretty lips surprised him. Cherry had gone from tense to total relaxation after one sip of her wine.

'I know now,' she said smugly.

'Oh do you, Miss Clever Clogs?' Angus was enjoying himself.

'You're in hospitality.'

His jaw dropped and he stared at her. 'What makes you say that?'

'You either work with food, or you sell food. Or maybe you're involved with the manufacture.' She picked up her snack pack and opened it before carefully placing it back on the tray. Her long slender fingers picked up a cracker, and then a slice of cheese went on top and then two raisins.

Angus's mouth dried as she lifted it to her lips and took a delicate bite.

'Well, am I right?'

He nodded. 'You are. What gave me away?'

This time her response was accompanied by an eye roll. 'Really? You don't know?'

'Apart from you jagging the right guess? No, I don't.'

'You are the only man I have seen pick up a packet of snacks and read the label. A dead giveaway. So what do you do exactly?' This time her lips were moist from the faint red of the rose she sipped.

As the soft musical notes of her laugh surrounded him, Angus wondered if he'd survive the remainder of the flight. 'That, my dear, is for me to know and you to find out.'

'I will,' she said firmly as she reached for another cracker and cheese.

***

Cherry couldn't believe how quickly the flight passed. Angus was still trying to guess what she did and she was enjoying the exchange, taking pleasure in watching the expressions change in his brown eyes, and then the movement of his lips as he smiled. His hands were graceful when he gestured with growing frustration as he moved through the medical professions: nurse, vet, dentist, and then through fashion: designer, dressmaker, model? His eyebrows lifted and were accompanied by a firm nod as he said "model".

'Uh, uh,' she said with a shake of her head. To Cherry's surprise, they were on their second glass of wine, but she didn't mind. She was feeling relaxed and mellow, and had even been able to bring herself to look down at the sea below. 'Look, you can see the white caps.'

Angus leaned across to look out the window and the warmth of his body touched her, and the fresh smell of his aftershave wafted over her. A warm feeling settled in her chest and she began to look forward to the next week. It was a small island, and surely—hopefully—they'd run into each other?

'You can. And look there.' He picked up her hand and directed her finger to a location at a forty-degree angle ahead of them. 'There's a ship. I wonder if it's the barge going out to the island. If it is, we're lucky to see it. Brad—my brother-in-law—said they waited for it every fortnight. It goes out from Port Macquarie and that's the only fresh produce they get. Apart from the bit they grow.'

'You know what?' Cherry replied. 'I think I could live like that. Away from the hectic pace of life and all the artificiality of being trendy and all that garbage.' Her voice was bitter and he wondered why. 'Could you?'

Angus swallowed and looked past her to the window again. He really couldn't answer that because that was one of the reasons he was on this flight. He'd learned a lot about the island from Brad and Sharon, and even though he hadn't read the tourist stuff, he knew how the island worked. He knew the climate, the population and the tourist numbers. His gut feeling already told him that it was too small for what he was looking for.

'So?'

He switched his attention back to Cherry. 'Sorry, what did you say?'

'Could you live on an island?'

'I don't know. Ask me on the flight back.'

In their conversation, they'd both been surprised to discover that they were travelling back on the same flight at the end of the week.

The captain's voice stopped Cherry from replying, and despite her two wines, Angus felt her stiffen beside him when the captain's voice came over the PA.

'Good afternoon, ladies and gentlemen. Please ensure your seatbelts are firmly fastened for landing. We've been watching the wind on the island, and it's picked up a bit of speed again over the past half hour, so we're going to circle around for a short time. Just to keep you informed, we have fifteen minutes to make a decision until we reach the point of no return with our fuel load, and if the wind strengthens in that time we'll be turning around and going back to Sydney. My apologies for the lack of information at this point, we'll let you know what's happening very soon. Cabin crew, please prepare cabin for landing.'

Angus looked down as Cherry grabbed his hand.

'I think I'm going to throw up.'

He let go of her hand and put his arm around her shoulder. 'It's okay. Take a deep breath. Remember what I said before. They are very experienced pilots. If it's safe to land they will. And if not we'll go back to Sydney, and get the next flight back.'

'Oh no. I won't be doing this again.' Her voice trembled. 'Once is enough.'

Disappointment flooded through Angus. He'd been looking forward to the next five days and getting to know Cherry better.

'You can't do that. I still don't know what you do for a living.'

This time her voice was flat. 'I'm in hospitality too.'

They sat quietly for a while, the only sound the roaring of the engines. The PA crackled again. 'Good news, ladies and gentlemen. The wind has dropped'—Cherry gasped as the aircraft banked sharply to the left—'and we are coming into land now. There's going to be a bit of turbulence, but we'll be on the tarmac soon.'

'Close your eyes and put your head on my shoulder, and we'll be on the island before you know it.' Angus kept his words low and confident, and before he could blink, Cherry's face turned into his shoulder. He stroked her arm gently as the plane bucked and swayed from side to side, and had to admit to a slight queasiness himself as they dropped suddenly and the pilot pulled the nose up. Almost immediately the tyres hit the tarmac, and the pilot engaged the reverse thrusters. With a roar, they were forced against their seatbelts and very quickly the plane braked and slowed.

The passengers broke into spontaneous applause, and Angus wondered how many times that happened at landing on the island. Maybe it was the norm, or maybe they'd just landed on a bad day of weather.

He looked down to the back of Cherry's head; her face was still pressed against him and her left hand was clutching his T-shirt.

'We're here,' he said softly. 'On the ground. Welcome to Lord Howe Island.'

She pulled back and her wide green eyes met his. 'Oh my God, I'm so sorry.' She brushed at his T-shirt with her fingers but he grabbed her hand and held it firmly. 'It's fine. We're just taxiing in and then we can get off.'

Before he knew what she was going to do, Cherry reached up and brushed her lips against his cheek. 'Thank you, Angus,' she said softly. 'You're a very kind man.'

At that moment Angus tumbled into love.

Chapter Eight

Pippa

At the end of the night, Tam and I left our respective partners in the bar, and headed for the kitchen. I linked my arm through hers when we reached the path.

'Happy with the meal? I thought everything was great.' I said as we walked past the beach. The last of the tenders was heading back to the catamarans moored out past our bay. It was a still night and I hoped that the calm weather continued to hold for the wedding in two weeks. The locals all said September was the best time up here. The winter south-easterlies had passed, and the wet season was still a few weeks off.

'Yes, each course was top quality, and the presentation was excellent. It seems our cranky duo managed to work together okay.' Tam stared ahead at the house. The veranda lights were off but there was still a glow coming from the kitchen at the back.

'It seems like it. Poor Mirabelle looked frazzled though, but every time I asked, she said everything was okay.'

'She worked hard, running to and fro from

the house to the bar. I told her to knock off and have a drink, but she said she was going straight to bed.'

I shook my head. 'She was probably worried that they'd come to the bar too. She's probably over them and wanted some space.'

'Could be. It'll be good when the Riccardos get the staff accommodation built up the hill. With our guys over from Hamo, and the new staff, it gets a bit crowded in the house.'

'Danny said as soon as the kitchen and restaurant is signed off, they'll make a start. Renzo's already had the surveyor up there and has pegged the buildings out.' I nudged Tam. 'Then you'll have some privacy when your man comes to stay.'

Tamsin chuckled. 'Poor Mirabelle's had a bad day. She didn't lock the bathroom door this morning and Gabe went in to have a shower. I don't know who was most embarrassed. He ended up going for a quick swim instead.'

'He'd have been more than embarrassed if he got stung in the water,' I said.

'I know. I tried to tell him, but he reckons it's safe enough.'

'That's my biggest worry with the resort. The sooner we get a pool in the better.'

'He and Nat were talking about rigging up an outside shower at the back of the shed where

Angus is bunking down. Would that be okay?'

'Sure, as a temporary measure, that's a great idea.' We'd reached the front house steps and looked at each other. 'Ready?'

Tam nodded and went up the steps first. 'Let's go see what's happening in there.'

When we walked into the kitchen, Cherry was standing at the sink, scrubbing a pot, but there was no sign of Angus.

'Almost done, Cherry?' Tamsin asked as I closed the screen door behind us.

'Yes. This is the last of it.' She turned around and I was struck by the change in her appearance. Her eyes were red as though she'd been crying and she looked miserable.

'Where's Angus?' I asked.

'I think he's gone to the bathroom.'

Tamsin walked over to the sink. 'You okay, love?'

Cherry nodded. 'Yes, just very embarrassed by what happened when we arrived. I'm really sorry. Honestly that's the first time I have ever done anything like that, but I got such a shock when I saw Angus.'

'I take it you worked together before?'

'No.' She bit her lip. 'I mean, yes, we both worked at Surfside for a while—Angus came after you left, but I was in the bar at a different hotel and he was in the kitchen.' She lifted her head. 'I suggested he applied there. We were already a couple when he started work.'

Tamsin's eyes widened. 'Oh.'

When footsteps sounded on the wooden boards of the veranda, Cherry turned back to the sink.

Angus pushed the door open. He'd changed into jeans and a T-shirt. Again—as I had when I'd first interviewed him—I thought what a good-looking man he was. He was tall and broad and filled out his white T-shirt very nicely. Not that I was checking him out, but a woman can appreciate a fine build, even if she was engaged.

'We just came up to tell you how good everything was,' I said as he stepped into the kitchen.

His usual smiling face was set, and his brow wrinkled in a frown. Finally he smiled and the laughter lines crinkled around his eyes. 'Thank you, Pippa. I was wondering about the sauce on the steaks. It's a new one I've been playing with. I probably shouldn't have tried it out on you tonight.'

'It was excellent,' Tamsin chimed in. 'Is that the one you mentioned you were going to put on the wedding menu?'

'Yes, one of them.' He flicked a glance over to the sink where Cherry was furiously scrubbing at the same pot. At the rate she was going it would be worn through. I looked back to Angus. 'Come down to the bar and join us for a drink. We'll be there for a while yet. You too, Cherry.'

Angus hesitated and shot another glance towards the sink.

'I won't take no for an answer. Come on, both of you,' I said with a smile. 'This is how we work on the island.'

Tamsin nodded. 'Yes. Come down and get to know the guys. Cherry, you go and get changed. I'll take over there.'

'I'm fine,' she said without turning around. 'I'm almost done here and I'm tired. I'll head to bed.'

'You've worked very hard tonight.' Angus walked over to the sink. 'I think you should come down too, please, Cherry. The boss has asked.' He lightened his words with a smile in my direction, but the smile seemed strained.

When Cherry turned it was hard to interpret her expression. It was a cross between confusion and resistance. She lifted her chin. 'Okay. For a short time.' Her back faced us again as she resumed her scrubbing. I raised my eyebrows at Tamsin and gestured to the door.

'Okay, we'll see you down there. Angus, have you both eaten?'

He shook his head. 'Ah, no.'

'Okay, we'll take some more nibbles down. The guys won't say no to more food.'

His brow creased in a frown. 'What? You're saying the meals weren't big enough?'

Tamsin hurried to reassure him. 'The meals were perfect. We have hungry men who would eat twenty-four seven.'

'You go back, and I'll put a basket together, and wait for . . . wait for Cherry.'

I was concerned when I saw her shoulders stiffen.

Angus must have picked up on it. 'Look we've worked all night without any yelling. I think we can last the rest of the night.'

'Okay, come on, Tam.'

We left, wondering if we had made a wise decision.

In more ways than one.

Chapter Nine

Lord Howe Island -2 years earlier

Cherry's legs were shaking as she walked down the four steps from the plane to the tarmac. Angus kept his hand beneath her elbow and she looked up at him gratefully. The wind was whipping his curls around his eyes, and his other hand was holding his carry-on bag. She reached up and tucked his hair behind his ear.

He grinned. 'Thank you. It was hard to see which way the terminal was.'

'It was the least I could do. You've looked after me since Sydney. I appreciate it. Very much.'

'No problems at all.' His hand firmed beneath her elbow. 'This way.'

A concrete path led from the tarmac to a low white picket fence enclosing an area of emerald green grass. Peeking over a grass-covered hill to the right was a cloud-topped mountain.

Cherry drew in her breath. 'Look at the colours of the water! The blues and the greens. How beautiful is this?' She grabbed for her long hair as it blew across her face. 'Despite the wind.'

Angus let go of her arm after they entered the small terminal building. 'You have luggage to collect, I guess?'

'I do. What about you?' Now that they had arrived the conversation was a little less relaxed. Almost as though he was keen to be rid of her, she thought.

He patted the soft bag slung over his shoulder. 'Nope, this is me done. I travel light.'

'Angus?' Cherry put her hand on his arm. 'Please don't feel as though you have to wait for me, or . . . or . . . look out for me now that we're here. I'm fine.'

His grin sent that warm feeling scurrying into her belly again. 'What if I want to? Wait for you, that is? *And* spend some time with you on the island.'

Cherry looked up at him from beneath her lashes. 'Really? You don't have to.' It was hard to believe that he wanted to; she was sure he was being polite.

'I think it would be much more fun to do the snorkelling and the walking and the fishing with a friend. What do you think?'

Her face heated. 'Um. Yes, it would be.'

The beeping of the luggage carousel starting up caught her attention.

'Which is your bag?' he asked as the suitcases began to appear.

She pointed as her bag came through the opening. 'That one. The olive green one.'

This time his grin was extra wide. 'Luggage to match your eyes and your shirt?'

Her face burned with embarrassment that he would think she was so vain. Folding her arms she looked up at him as they waited for the bag to come closer. 'No, luggage that was on special at Pacific Fair!'

'I was joking.'

He reached for the bag, but she protested. You don't have to carry mine too.'

'My mother taught me to be a gentleman. Come and we'll find the bus that takes us to our lodges.'

It appeared that over half of the passengers on the plane were locals returning home as they were met by family with cars parked near the minibus that was waiting in the car park.

The driver jumped out and came around to open the back to stow the bags as they crossed towards the bus.

'Welcome, welcome to Lord Howe Island,' he said to Angus and Cherry and the other two couples who came across to the bus. 'I'm Ronny, and I'll be taking you to your lodges.' He pulled out a clipboard and scanned the names. 'I have the Bakers, the Millers, one Alexander and one Chilcott. Excellent, you're all staying in lodges on Ned's Beach Road.' He took the various suitcases and stowed them in the back. 'Great choice! This way, folks.' Ronny pulled open the sliding door and Angus stood back to let the two couples and Cherry board the bus first. She was pleased she was on first because she didn't want to have to make the decision of whether to sit by herself or next to Angus if he'd got on first. As it was, he swung himself into the empty seat beside her.

'So we're here safely. On the ground on Lord Howe Island,' he said stowing his bag between his feet.

Ronny yelled from the driver's seat. 'Did you all enjoy the landing? It was fun to watch.'

Cherry rolled her eyes and muttered quietly. 'It wasn't fun to be on.'

There were mumbles of agreement from the other two couples and she didn't feel so bad, but she jumped when Angus reached over and took her hand and squeezed it. 'I'm going to teach you to be a risk taker this week.'

Cherry blushed as all sorts of inappropriate thoughts went through her mind. She sat straight and looked at him, hardly believing the flirting comment that flew from her mouth. 'That might be just what I need.'

***

Angus looked across at Cherry as the minibus took them along the front of a sapphire-blue lagoon. Small boats bobbed on the gentle swell that came across from the reef, but in the distance, the strong wind that was still bending the palm trees had whipped up the white breakers that crashed on the reef protecting the lagoon.

'It's really beautiful, isn't it?' She turned and looked at him. 'I had no idea those colours were real. I thought the tourist brochures had been touched up, but it's their true colour.'

'I think that's one of the lagoons where there's snorkelling trips.' He held her gaze. 'Have you ever gone snorkelling or scuba diving?'

'No, I've never really been a water person. I'm lucky if I can work up the courage to go underwater in a swimming pool.' Cherry shook her head and her long hair brushed his arm. 'Like I said, I'm not a risk taker. I'm pretty boring.'

Angus had never been so fascinated by a woman before, and he couldn't understand exactly why. He'd been out with beautiful women, but he'd never felt this deep attraction. It was hard to explain; it wasn't a sexual attraction, but was coming from somewhere deeper within. Maybe it was because he saw himself in the role of rescuer, and it made him feel good about himself.

All Angus knew was that he wanted to keep

looking at Cherry, wanted to spend time with her and see her happy and smiling.

Ronny called over his shoulder. 'This is the main lagoon, folks, and we're about to turn into Ned's Beach Road where you're all staying. In a couple of hours, if you walk to the other side of the island, you can see the fish feed at Ned's Beach. I guarantee once you see it, you'll be back there every afternoon. Then if you stay over there until sunset, you'll see the mutton birds fly back to their nests. There might not be a lot of organised entertainment on our island, but nature puts on all the shows for you. Make sure you read the brochures in your rooms and try everything we have to offer. I guarantee you won't be sorry, and I'll also bet that you'll come back to our island.'

Angus leaned forward. 'That covers the days, thanks, Ronny. Which restaurant would you recommend for the best meal at night?'

At first it seemed he was quite the diplomatic guide. 'Hmm, I can't really recommend one over the other, because they're all good.' He shook his head and then lowered his voice. 'Now don't quote me on this because I could be run off the island, but if you're a steak lover, you can't go past Trader Bob's.'

'Thank you. I'm a steak man.' Angus nodded. That was what he'd wanted to hear, but he still wasn't sure about moving to such a small island.

Cherry touched his arm and the nerve endings from head to toe kicked in. 'If you love your steak, would you let me take you there one night'—she stumbled over her words—'to um, to ah, say thank you for being so kind to me.'

'Yes, that would be great. I'd love that,' he replied.

She held his gaze with those beautiful green eyes and it was very hard for him to look away. He couldn't explain it. Looking at Cherry made him feel different. But a good different.

The moment was broken by Ronny calling over his shoulder as the bus lurched to a stop. 'This is Sunset Lodge. Ms Chilcott, this is your lodge.'

Angus stood so Cherry could get out of the seat, and before he sat again, he said, 'I'll come back in a couple of hours and walk to the beach with you, if you'd like to see the fish feeding?'

'That would be nice.' Her smile was pretty and hit him in the gut like a sucker punch.

What the hell is wrong with me?

Chapter Ten

Cherry - Lord Howe Island

It didn't take Cherry long to unpack. Her room at Sunset Lodge was basic but clean, and it suited her needs. The bedroom had a double bed with a table and lamp on each side, there was no kitchen, and a table between the bedroom and the small living room, held a toaster and a kettle. The front veranda looked out over a green lawn surrounded by colourful hibiscus bushes, and at the edge of the lawn on a tennis court behind a high wire fence, an energetic game was in progress.

On the way to her room, once she'd checked in and collected her key, Cherry had passed an outdoor cooking area surrounded by some hammock chairs that looked perfect for reading and relaxing. Although it seemed that Angus had plans for filling their days with lots of physical activity; it appeared that her holiday was going to be different to what she'd planned.

But really, when Cherry thought about it, she'd had no plan, and no desire to see or do anything in particular. The whole holiday had been a kneejerk reaction to her family. She flopped into the soft chair on the veranda as she thought about her decision to come here.

Strangely it was beginning to have a positive spin and the decision to take a holiday appeared to have been a good one. The horrendous plane flight was behind her, and she would ignore the fact that she had to get on a plane and go home in five days.

Meeting Angus had had a huge impact on her. It had been a long time since anyone had been so kind to her, and shown an interest in her.

And it felt good. She felt as if she could be herself with him. Her shyness had disappeared, and she was looking forward to seeing him again later.

But, she bit her lip, she didn't want to appear needy. She'd spend some of the days doing things by herself.

It was time to take control and not let her actions and behaviour be driven by her reactions to situations. If the truth be known, she *was* boring, but it was because she'd let herself become that way.

It was a family expectation that that was how she'd act and react, and that was what she'd always done. Reacted to expectations.

No more.

The way Angus had helped her today, and looked out for her wellbeing had woken something in her, and she'd never had that happen to her before. Suddenly she felt full of life, and wanted to squeeze every bit of enjoyment she could out of this holiday.

Slowly, slowly, she warned herself.

Enjoy his company, and enjoy the time away from work and all that was familiar.

Don't go reading too much into one good man being kind to you.

When she got back to the Gold Coast, she would examine every aspect of her life, and she'd start making more of an effort to do what *she* wanted to do, and to be happier. She would try to get out of that bar job, and chase up a course that might help her get into the food side of hospitality.

I can do it, she thought to herself.

I can do it! The affirmation would go up on her fridge so she saw it every morning.

But in the meantime she was going to plunge head first into this holiday, push out of her comfort zone and have a great time.

If Lord Howe Island was first step in her journey to happiness and contentment, and changing her mindset, maybe . . . it was thanks to Angus. Their interactions so far may have been brief, but he had made her think and feel.

Cherry put her head back on the soft cushion, smiled and closed her eyes.

An hour later, she woke up with a start; she *never* slept in the daytime, but she'd gone out like a light as soon as she'd put her head on the soft back of this comfy chair. Jumping up, she hurried into the bathroom, took a quick shower, brushed her hair and pulled it back into a high ponytail. Standing in front of the cupboard where she'd unpacked her clothes, she put one hand to her mouth and frowned.

What did you wear to fish feeding? Cherry's choice was limited because she'd not brought many clothes with her. She pulled out a pair of shorts and a clean T-shirt.

After slipping her denim shorts on, Cherry went to pull the T-shirt over her head, but hesitated. It was warm outside, so she pulled on a white singlet top instead and covered it with a light sleeveless blue shirt that she tied in a knot at her waist.

A smear of lip gloss, a pair of dangly earrings and her white Skechers, and she was ready to go.

Tucking her room key into her pocket, she headed out to the front of the lodge. She passed a few other guests and everyone smiled and stopped for a brief chat.

'How long have you been here?'

'Just arrived.'

'Are you staying long?' She shook her head.

'Are you going fishing?'

'Maybe.'

'Are you climbing the mountain?'

She responded with a big smile. 'I hope so.'

The island had a great feel about it so far. Even Ronny, the bus driver, had been extra welcoming. Maybe Mum and Dad had been right about the island.

Angus was waiting at the end of the driveway and Cherry couldn't help basking in the appreciative look in his eyes as he watched her walk towards him.

'Good to see you dressed ready to go in the water,' he said as he reached for her hand. It seemed natural to let his fingers curl around hers, and she didn't remove her hand.

'Have you got your dollar?' he asked tapping his shirt pocket with his free hand.

'My dollar? What for?' Cherry frowned trying to remember any mention of money from the brochure. 'Do I need money?'

'To feed the fish.' He chuckled. 'Did you read the compendium in your room?'

'No. I took a nap.'

'Well, you sure do look refreshed.'

Cherry held his gaze as he reached up and touched her cheek. 'Much more colour in your face now. You've got a rosy glow.'

'I'm feeling good. What did you do?'

'I spent the time reading. And it's okay, I

brought a spare dollar for you. I had a feeling you might have a rest. That flight was pretty draining.'

'I'll owe you.'

'The compendium has all sort of activities. There's heaps to do here.' His voice was filled with enthusiasm. 'How fit are you?'

'Hmm. I don't work out at the gym, if you meant that sort of fit?'

'Not quite, but there's a couple of climbs I'd like to do. One's a bit challenging.'

'You're the one who said I should start to be a risk taker, so that might be the way to start. Stretch my boundaries a bit.'

'We'll make a schedule later. How's your room?'

'Basic, but functional. I think I might have the low end of the market. What about yours?'

'Same. But you know what I like best?'

'What's that?' They were almost to the end of the road and Cherry could see the beach ahead.

'Digital silence. There's no phone service: no internet, so no social media updates . . . absolute quiet.'

'I imagine some people would find that very hard, but I won't miss it. I don't go online much.'

'I agree, but look what replaces it. Perfect scenery, pure white sand, incredibly blue water, coral that we can swim out to, and dozens of different walks to choose from every day, not to mention a selection of restaurants for dinner.'

'You're exhausting me.' Cherry bit her lip and looked up at him. 'Seriously though, Angus. I do like being with you, but please don't feel as though you have to look after me, or keep me entertained. I'm fine in my own company.'

'No, seriously, you're doing me a favour. I hate being by myself. I had enough of that on our cattle property growing up.'

'So you're a social person?'

'When I want to be.'

She stared at him and frowned. 'So how come you came on a solo holiday? Not on a tour or with a friend—or a girlfriend?'

Okay, so she might be shamelessly digging, but she liked him. *Really* liked him.

And that was something new for her, recently anyway. Not going out much these days meant she didn't meet new people. It had been a while since Cherry had had a relationship of any sort with a guy. Not even friendships. And that meant she was unsure of what was required from her. How to act, what to say, without giving the wrong impression.

'None of the above, he said. 'I came here to find something out, but I'll tell you about that later. Look, we're here now, let's go feed these fish.'

They reached the crest at the end of the narrow road and a curved bay stretched out in front of them. Angus was right; the water was blue and the sand was white. A group of tourists waited on the water's edge and as they watched a man walked down with a large bucket in each hand.

'Look,' said Cherry pointing to the beach. 'It's Ronny, our bus driver.'

'I guess on an island this small, we'll see that often,' Angus said. 'He confessed to me when I was last off the bus, that he is a waiter at the restaurant he recommended. I guess he was feeling guilty.'

The fish feeding was great fun. Nothing like feeding goldfish-sized fish like Cherry had expected, but it involved throwing pellets and bread scraps and fish frames to the massive kingfish that came rocketing in around their legs when they tossed the food in the water. For their size, the fish were incredibly tame, but energetic. At one point her legs were surrounded by dozens of silver fish.

'Hang on,' Angus yelled as an extra-large kingfish headed to the beach and pushed against Cherry's legs. She teetered and was almost knocked off her feet. Angus grabbed her, his hands firm against her waist. She giggled as a great whoosh of water soaked them both, and was very pleased that she had a loose shirt on that covered her now wet and clinging singlet top.

The best part was, Angus stayed behind her with his arms around her, holding her steady as the huge fish swam around their legs. Ripples of warmth shot through Cherry and settled deep.

She was disappointed when Ronny picked up his buckets. 'That's it for today, folks. Make sure you come back and snorkel here at high tide tomorrow. There's a beautiful dive out there with fish and corals along a fringing coral reef. We have the southernmost coral reef in the world.' He gave them a wave and headed up the beach, followed by the rest of the group who had come to watch the fish feeding.

'Can we come back tomorrow?' she asked Angus with a wide grin. 'And do it again?'

'Sure can.' He looked like he'd enjoyed it as much as she had. 'Look at that.' He pointed to a sign as they walked off the beach carrying their shoes. 'The masks and snorkels and fins are all there, and there's an honesty box system.'

'Wow, it's like going back in time, isn't it? I can't imagine that on the Gold Coast.'

'That's where you live?' he asked with a smile.

'It is. What about you?'

'The Gold Coast.' His eyes held hers and crinkled in a smile.

Cherry didn't let her hopes get up; maybe she'd see him again when they went home.

Slowly, slowly.

'What's next?' she asked.

Angus pointed to the small forest that edged the beach. 'Apparently this island is the only breeding place for these birds in eastern Australia. Ronny gave me a running commentary before I got off the bus.'

'Sounds like you got the full tourist spiel,' she said with a grin.

'I did. He assures me it will be a spectacular sight, so we sit and wait for dusk. Apparently this side is the best place to see the mutton birds come back to the island for the night.' He looked around. 'It looks like we're the only ones here this afternoon.' Angus held out his hand. 'He said the ground is uneven and to watch out for hidden burrows.'

Stepping into the dim palm forest with Angus holding her hand was the last thing Cherry would have expected on this holiday. The forest was pleasantly cool after the heat of the late afternoon sun on the beach. Most of the ground was sandy and uneven with long furrows obvious, but there were sections of soft green grass that were cool beneath her feet and she shivered.

'Would you rather go back and get dry

clothes on? We can see this another afternoon,'
Angus asked.

'No, I'm fine. I'm not that wet.'

He laughed. 'You reckon?'

Cherry followed his gaze down to the front of her shirt. She hadn't realised that the knot around her waist had come undone, and her wet singlet top was in full view; being chilled made it a *very* interesting view.

Heat ran into her face and she grabbed the sides of the shirt and reknotted them.

'Spoilsport.' His grin was cheeky and Cherry pulled a face at him.

'Come and sit over here. There's a little bit of sun coming through the leaves, and we can get a good view of the birds coming in. When Ronny dropped me off, he told me where to sit too.' He led her to a huge log that had fallen. 'Careful, watch out for the nests.'

She looked up but he shook his head and pointed down. 'That's what those long indented bits are in the sand. The mutton birds burrow in the sand. The burrows are about two metres long and they dig a little chamber at the end. One bird stays with the eggs while the other one goes out to sea to collect food through the day, and they fly in at dusk.'

Cherry was enjoying hearing the local

knowledge that Angus had picked up already. 'Like I said, it's very different to home, isn't it?'

They settled in the middle of the log where a gap in the palm forest gave them a good view of the beach and the bay. Angus left a space between them after Cherry had sat down. 'I hope you don't think I was assuming too much, but I asked Ronny to reserve a table for two at the restaurant at eight? If you'd rather do something else that's fine. I can go by myself.' She chuckled as he put on a sad face.

'That's fine with me, but remember, it's my shout.'

'We'll see,' was all he said.

They sat quietly, and the silence was companionable as they listened to the sounds in the forest. The leaves rustled in the stiff breeze, and the occasional creak of a bough made Cherry smile. 'That sound always reminds me of that lullaby. I used to sing it to my dolls when I was little. I always wondered how they got the baby's cradle up there.'

'I don't know that one,' Angus said.

'Rock-a-bye baby?' She looked at him and shook her head. 'Really?'

He laughed. 'Really. I must have missed out on that part of growing up. But do you know what? I'm really pleased I took this trip. I'm really loving it here already.' Angus looked out across the bay. It

was as though he was half speaking to himself, so
Cherry didn't answer. 'I wonder if I could live
somewhere this quiet?'

Chapter Eleven

Angus – Lord Howe Island

The mutton birds came into the island as the sun set. A huge swathe of black cut across the dusky pink sky. Soon the air was filled with mournful wails as the birds headed for their nests and burrowed in for the night.

Angus looked down at Cherry; her eyes were wide as she moved her head from left to right watching the hundreds of birds that settled in the forest around them. Her cheeks were flushed and her lips were open and she oohed and aahed as the birds disappeared into their burrows in the sand. The surge of desire that hit him was not unexpected. He'd found it hard to stop looking at her since the wet T-shirt incident. He couldn't get over how natural she was. Her beauty was stunning: her face, her eyes, her lips, her body, the whole damn package was gorgeous.

But she played no games; and if he was reading her correctly, Cherry was totally unaware of how attractive she was. He'd even noticed old Ronny, who was probably on the wrong side of seventy, looking at her a few times as they'd fed the kingfish on the beach.

'We may as well not even be here,' she said, oblivious to the heat sizzling through his bloodstream. She looked up at him and smiled, and his heart rate notched up.

'I guess the mutton birds are used to people being on the island. And never feel threatened,' Angus replied, forcing his eyes away from her.

'I've never seen anything like it,' she said shaking her head.

'Or heard,' Angus added.

'It's a bit noisy.'

He gestured towards the road. 'Are you ready to go back?'

When she nodded, he stood and held out his hand. 'I don't know about you but I'm starving.'

'Did you have any lunch? I noticed you didn't eat those delectable snacks on the plane.'

'Actually no. I intended going to that shop we passed and getting some fruit and stuff for my room, but I got reading the tour guide and ran out of time. What about you?'

'No.' She shook her head. 'But I am hungry. I'll enjoy my dinner.'

Angus nodded slowly as they walked along the road. 'I hope we do. It'll be interesting.'

'That's a strange way to talk about dinner. How do you mean *interesting*?'

'I've got a confession to make. I have a

reason for being on the island. Apart from a bit of a holiday.'

'A reason?' She tipped her head to the side.

'Yeah, I've been offered a job here, and I wanted to come and check out the island and the restaurant anonymously. I'm a chef.'

'Ah. And what do you think so far? Although we haven't really been here long enough to judge the place fairly.'

Angus hesitated for a moment. 'Honestly? Okay, I think what we've seen so far is beautiful, but I don't know if I could live and work here. Now I know why they were insisting on a two-year contract, plus a paid trip back to the mainland every six months. I'd say they might find it hard to keep staff. I could be wrong though.'

'Maybe once you'd seen everything here, and done all the climbs and the walks, it *could* get a bit boring. That is, if you like busy places, or if you like to socialise.'

'The Gold Coast has a vibe, that's for sure, but apart from the occasional surf or game of golf, I don't really do anything or go out much. Hospitality hours are a killer for a social life.'

'They are.' She put her head to the side and observed him. 'The quiet of this island really appeals to me. A person could come over here and hide.'

'It'd be fairly hard to hide on a piece of rock this small. I reckon your business would be known as soon as you stepped off the plane. You know what small towns are like. Well, this is even smaller.' He looked at her as curiosity surfaced. 'What would you want to hide from anyway?'

Her sigh seemed to come from the depths of her soul. 'Life. Family. Expectations.'

'Work?' he asked.

'I don't mind working,' she said.

'What do you do, Cherry?'

'Me?' She shrugged and he found it hard to keep his eyes off the bare skin of her shoulders. 'I do a bit of casual work in the hospitality industry. So I do understand what you meant by the hours.'

'Waitressing? Or kitchen work?' He shook his head. 'I'm sorry. That was a sexist assumption to make. A chef?'

'No. Not a chef. Sometimes a waitress, but mostly bar work.'

'On the coast?'

'Yes. I've worked in a few different places.' Her answers seemed vague and Angus sensed she was being evasive, but he persisted. 'What part of the coast?'

'At Tweed Heads for a while, and I've been at Surfside lately. The one near Southport.'

'Really? Well, I'll be damned.'

'Why?' They'd reached the driveway of the Sunset Lodge, and stopped on the lush green grass. The thwack of tennis balls and laughter drifted across from the tennis court on the other side of the narrow road.

'As well as the job here, I've been offered a sous chef job at Surfside on Broadwater,' Angus said. 'I'll pick your brains over dinner and you can tell me what it's like as a workplace. Double bonus… you can tell me the difference between Trader Bob's and Surfside. I have a feeling they are two very different establishments.'

'Sounds like you've got some decisions to make, but I'm not really the person to help. I haven't worked in the restaurant much. I probably can't help at all really.' Cherry took a step away from him.

'Fair enough. How long do you need to get ready? We could have a drink at one of the other restaurants before we walk around to Trader Bob's. Unless you'd prefer to go in the island taxi?'

'I'm happy to walk. And a drink first sounds like a plan. I'll have another quick shower to get the salt water off me, so say half an hour?'

Angus blocked the thought of Cherry in the shower totally out of his mind. Or as best he could, anyway.

***

Cherry dug into her suitcase. Shorts, T-shirts, jeans, a couple of dressy tops and the obligatory black dress—she had totally misjudged packing for the island.

She dropped the dress on top of the pile of casual gear. The dress was fairly dressy, and she was getting a sense that the island was pretty laid back.

So, dress or jeans?

Cherry stood in front of the mirror and held the black dress up in front of her, and then turned to her jeans and tops. The dressiest jeans were the white ones that she'd worn on the plane today, and she'd rinsed them in the shower and hung them over the chair to dry before they'd gone to feed the fish.

She felt them and pulled a face; they were still too damp to wear.

So it was the faded denims or the dress. With a sigh, she glanced at her watch on the table and realised she'd have to get a move on. It was ten before seven and Angus had said he'd come and collect her at her unit at seven.

She pulled the dress on over her head and smoothed her hands over it to get the wrinkles out. Slipping flat sandals on, she hurried back into the bathroom to do her hair and put a tiny bit of makeup on. Quickly braiding her hair, Cherry pinched her cheeks and was ready just as there was a tap on the screen door.

Chapter Twelve

Pippa -Pentecost Island
One week before the wedding

'Sweetheart?'

I stood at the window staring out over the brilliant blue waters of the Whitsunday Passage. The view from Rafe's kitchen was incredible and I never tired of looking at it. He'd laughed at me two weeks after I moved in with him when I refused to use the dishwasher. I preferred standing at the sink looking at the incredible view to the west as I washed the dishes by hand.

'Sweetheart?' Rafe repeated and I turned as the concern in his voice cut through my daydreaming. He had come into the kitchen without me hearing him. His fingers were white where they gripped the edge of the benchtop. I hurried across to him and grabbed his arm.

'What's wrong? Are you ill?' I stared up at his face, and for the first time I noticed the straight line of his set lips. 'Are you all right?' He looked to be in pain.

He nodded slowly, but his expression remained grave. 'I'm well.'

'Well, what's the matter?'

'I've had some bad news.'

I drew in my breath as he let me lead him into the living room, and pull him down onto the sofa. 'What is it? What's happened?'

All I could think of was it was something that was going to impact on us, and mean the cancellation of our wedding.

I'd always known it was too good to be true. My life had taken such a dramatic turn around since Aunty Vi had left me half the island, and I'd met and fallen in love with Rafe.

'I had a phone call from England.'

Tears sprang unbidden to my eyes and I brushed them away angrily. I'd survived a lot in my life and I wasn't going to let him see how much he could hurt me. Maybe I was being selfish, but it just wasn't fair. Memories of Darren, my ex, surfaced and I pushed them away. No, Rafe wasn't a bit like that. He loved me and he wouldn't let me down.

Gentle hands took mine and I stared down at Rafe's hands as I realised how cold they were. Whatever the call had been, it had upset him.

Deeply.

'We can't get married? Your ex-wife called?' I kept my voice as light as I could, despite the pain knifing though me.

'Oh, sweetheart, no. It's got nothing to do with us or the wedding. I would never let anything stop us getting married.' He lifted his hands and cupped my face as another tear threatened to fall. 'Phillipa. Look at me. You have to learn to trust me. I won't let you down.'

'I'm sorry. I'm a selfish bitch. Tell me what's wrong.'

'You're not. I know what you've been through. I shouldn't have made you worry. It's Jenny and Bryant. They can't come to the wedding. There's been an accident and their daughter is in hospital.'

'Oh, I'm sorry.' I leaned against him and put my head on his shoulder. 'I know how much you were looking forward to them being here. And Bryant was going to be your best man! Is their daughter badly hurt?'

'A whiplash injury, but she's fine. Apparently Odessa is pretty fragile; she was in the passenger seat and her friend who was driving, was killed in the accident.'

'Oh, that's so sad. And I feel bad for you too, Rafe. They were the only guests coming for you.'

'I'll survive. As long as you marry me in eight more days, I don't care who's there. I just worry about Jenny and Bryant. Odessa hasn't been the easiest child for them; she's led a pretty wild life. I looked out for her when she was in her teens.

She used to talk to me, and sometimes I was able to keep her on the straight and narrow.' He pulled a face. 'But sometimes not.'

'You were close to her?'

'I was.'

'How old is she now?'

'About your age.'

'Oh.' A niggle of jealousy surfaced. There was so much about Rafe I didn't know, and I wondered if I was making yet another mistake in my life. God knows, there's been plenty of them.

'Phillipa?

'Um, yes?' I looked up and his dark eyes were intent on mine.

'Listen to me.' He articulated each word slowly in that sexy posh accent I loved so much. 'Do. Not. Doubt. My Love. For. You. Stop overthinking and putting that fertile imagination of yours to work.' His hands held my shoulders and he lowered his head and his forehead rested against mine. 'You are the woman I love. You are the woman I am marrying in eight days, and you are the woman I am going to spend the rest of my life with.'

'I'm sorry. And I'm sorry about what's happened. You're a good man. Would you like to bring our trip forward and go over after the wedding so you can see them? Make sure they're okay?'

'No, we'll stick to our original plan. Bryant assures me they'll be fine. They're staying home; Odessa was released from hospital last week, and they've decided not to leave her alone. They suggested that maybe she could come out here for a holiday in a while. Thank you for offering to do that, sweetheart, but there's too much going on here for us to leave early.' He moved away from me, stood up and held out his hand. 'Speaking of which, I want to show you something. I was about to call you when the phone rang.'

'What? Is something else wrong?' I kept hold of his hand after I stood.

'No, something else is very right. Just be patient and come with me. It will make you extremely happy.'

'How do you know? What is it?'

'Because I went for a walk early this morning while you were snoring in our bed.'

I squeezed his fingers. 'I don't snore.'

'Well, it was a pretty snuffle then.'

'So what is it we're going to look at? Has Evie finished the garden around the lawn where we're doing our vows?'

Rafe smiled and shook his head. 'Patience, Phillipa.' Before we turned to the door, he pulled me close and brushed his lips across mine.

I whispered against his mouth. 'Just as well

116

I love you so much.'

'How much?' His words vibrated against my lips.

'To the moon and back. Forever.'

Chapter Thirteen
Cherry

'Where would you like me to put the large pots?' Cherry asked politely. She hadn't been able to use his name when addressing Angus; it brought back too many memories and strangely, it seemed as though it would be too intimate. They were the only two in the new kitchen, so there was no doubt that she was talking to him.

Angus stared at her. 'In the pot drawer next to the main cooker, of course.' His tone implied that it had been a stupid question.

'I was referring to the new pots.' She kept her expression as bland as her tone. 'Some of them are large. Possibly too big for that drawer, do you think?'

He lifted his eyebrows and stared at her without speaking. Cherry nodded and went back to her task. She would do as she was told, and if they wouldn't fit , he could sort it. Tamsin had called in briefly, and after a quick look at what was in the boxes, had told Angus to arrange it to suit his needs for the time being. Cherry could not afford to let her simmering temper—a temper she'd never known existed until now—ignite.

Yes, sir. No sir. Three bags full, sir. She was getting better at learning to stay calm the more they worked together. And if she was honest, she had already learned a lot by watching Angus working in the kitchen each night. Reluctantly she admitted to herself, he would make an excellent teacher.

Sometimes she could even forget what he had done, but only for short times; if only they didn't have a personal history, this would be the perfect job.

Sometimes when he looked at her, his expression was hard to read. The early anger seemed to have disappeared, as though he had accepted the situation too, but his tone often indicated that he was uneasy.

Well, buddy, you'll have to deal with it, Cherry thought.

She was, but she was keeping Angus' previous treatment of her to the forefront of her thoughts. Liking your boss was not a prerequisite for any workplace. Being respectful and doing what you were told, was.

She would do it, no matter how unreasonable and cranky Angus was. He was the one who would sign her off in the long run, and she would last the distance.

No matter what.

Cherry had not put a foot wrong. If Angus had told her to pour boiling oil down the sink, she would have done so and her tone would have remained icily polite as it had for the past few days. She was going to complete this traineeship and if it meant jumping through the hoops that Angus Alexander put in front of her, she would do it.

She was a much stronger person than she had been eighteen months ago. Ironically, both Angus' love and betrayal had taught her to be so. Whatever it took, she would deliver. Gritting her teeth she unpacked the new copper based pots and placed them in the centre of the large drawer beside the gas cooker.

When she attempted to close the drawer, and it wouldn't shut, she didn't speak. Angus was over near the cavernous walk-in pantry, as she attempted to rearrange the pots. They were too big to fit, but she tried every arrangement so Angus wouldn't have a reason to criticise her.

'Have you almost finished there? There's another box of pans here.' The tone of his voice replicated hers. Icily polite, no emotion and for the first time, there was a hint of patience.

'Almost, but the larger pots won't fit.'

Angus strode over. Cherry wasn't quick

enough to step back before he reached around her, rearranged the medium pots and tried to push the largest one into the space he'd created. She didn't say a word; she'd already tried that. The trouble was, she still had hold of the largest one. When he reached for it, their fingers entwined around the handle together. Angus jumped back as though he'd been burnt, and Cherry did the same and the pot clattered on top of the others. She mumbled something unintelligible and looked down, but she knew he was looking at her.

And that he was looking at her in the way that he had in the past. She didn't have to see, she could feel the emotion coming off him.

For the first time since Cherry had arrived, she realised that Angus was not immune to her either.

Walking across to the boxes that were yet to be unpacked, she hid a smile when he picked up the offending pan and put it on the countertop.

***

I was getting used to the sound of hammers and saws on the island, and it was easy to put up with the constant noise because I knew it was moving us closer to the culmination of my dream every day. I hadn't seen the progress of the work for a couple of days. Yesterday Rafe and I had gone over to Hamo in his boat, and met with the celebrant who was coming over to our island next weekend.

The builders had already begun, even though it was early, and I was surprised when Rafe led me along the beach path and we entered the work site from the southern end. Music came from ahead of us, a soft rock piece and as we moved through the trees I could hear someone singing along with it.

'The day spa!' Excitement fizzed through me. 'That's Sienna's voice.' We stepped out of the forest and I drew in a breath. 'Oh my goodness, it's beautiful.'

Sienna appeared in the doorway, her hands clasped to her chest, and a wide smile lighting up her face. 'They finished it yesterday, Pippa, while you were away. Come and see. It's absolutely gorgeous.'

Rafe and I followed her into the spacious hut, and I looked around in amazement. The smell of fresh paint was overlaid with a soft floral fragrance that was drifting out of an oil diffuser. But it was the interior that made me smile.

Not only was the building finished, but it was already fully fitted out. The soft furnishings were in place, the royal blue curtains moved in the gentle breeze off the bay, and Sienna's products lined the timber shelves.

She opened the curtain that divided the hut into two discrete sections. 'Look.'

In the smaller room that faced the water, the two treatment beds were side by side and covered with royal blue coverlets.

'Oh my God!' I shook my head. 'It looks like it's ready to begin.'

Sienna nodded with excitement. 'Danny has to finish off the plumbing in the en suite, and then yes, it's ready to go.'

I knew my eyes were wide as I took it all in. 'When did you do all of this? I didn't even know you'd ordered your products.'

'Sienna and I did it on the quiet so it would be a surprise for your wedding.'

I turned as Eliza came into the room. 'I'm gobsmacked,' I said.

'It was pretty easy to keep it under wraps

because you've been so busy with your wedding plans, and keeping an eye on the situation in the kitchen.'

I walked over and hugged Sienna. 'Thank you so much.'

She smiled, and nodded. 'We worked hard to have it ready for the wedding party makeup next Saturday. I'd like to have a practice go with you tomorrow. Would you have time?'

'I'll make time.'

Rafe called over to me. 'There's one more thing for you to see.'

'I'm coming too.' Eliza linked her arm through mine. 'I want to see your face.'

'Me too,' said Sienna as she and Rafe followed us out.

'So where to now?' I asked.

'You'll see.' Rafe caught up to us and stood behind me. 'Close your eyes.'

I laughed and did as he bid. He took my other hand and he and Eliza led me along the path.

'No peeking,' she said.

The noise of the builder's tools had stopped, and the only sound was the soft music from the day spa, but that faded as they led me along. The sharp call of a bird surrounded us and I heard its wings beat as it took off from close to where we walked.

'Keep them closed.' Rafe's hands were on

my shoulders now as he steered me to the left. I heard a door open, then he said, 'Up one step.'

Again I did as I was told.

Silence.

'Okay, you can open your eyes now.'

It took a moment for my vision to adjust to the dim interior, and I realised we were in the restaurant.

'Surprise!'

My bottom lip quivered with emotion as I looked around. 'Oh my freaking God! Did you guys work all night?'

Tamsin and Nell were across the room next to the bar, and Evie and Jed were sitting at a table. Angus was standing in the doorway that led to the kitchen, and Cherry was at the other end of the bar.

'We worked all day yesterday, and yes, into the night,' Tamsin said as she walked across to us.

'Do you guys know how much I love you?' My voice choked up as I looked around the restaurant. The tables were laid with white linen cloths, the glassware and cutlery sparkled, the bar shelves had been filled with bottles from the storeroom—we'd decided to keep the outside bar as a casual bar—and the restaurant was ready for the guests as far as I could see.

'We do,' Tamsin said tugging at my hand. 'But not as much as I love those Riccardo men.

Come and see the kitchen. I just can't believe it, Pip. It's amazing.'

I was almost in a state of shock. Rafe and I had left the island for one day and two of the major buildings were complete. 'How the heck did you get this all done on one day?'

Nell smiled. 'When we knew you were going to Hamo, we suggested to Rafe that you stay for dinner, and make it a long day. Once he'd organised that, we told Danny and Renzo and they tripled their work crews for the day. Then we all came in late last night and put the gloss on everything.'

'I owe you all.'

Tamsin tugged at my hand again, and when I went with her, Angus and Cherry followed us into the kitchen. I glanced at them; they kept their distance from each other but everything seemed okay. I'd called into the old kitchen a few times unannounced over the last week, and it appeared that they had made their peace.

Well, at least there hadn't been any knives in evidence.

Gleaming banks of stainless steel met me. Pots and pans hung above the two big gas cookers, and everything seemed to be in place. There were a couple of boxes of produce on the countertop near the sink waiting to be unpacked.

'When you have a moment, Pippa, Angus and I would like to meet with you,' Tamsin said. 'We've got some ideas and a few questions.'

'How about now? After I finish the grand tour.' I glanced at Rafe. 'Unless you had some plans, love?'

He shook his head. 'No, I'll go back up to the house. I've got some more calls to make. I had the tour before.'

I turned and looked at my friends. Only Philippe, Nat and Gabe were missing. 'Thank you, all. I'm . . . I'm speechless.'

'That'd be a first, wouldn't it, Tam?' Nell said with a wide grin. 'Pippa can't find anything to say.'

'I can. I think this calls for a party,' I said.

Eliza stepped forward. 'Ah, sweetie, did you forget? We're having a big nosh up next Saturday. Someone's getting married.'

'Well, how about sunset drinks tonight? On the beach.'

There were nods all round.

'The kitchen staff can take it in shifts,' Tamsin directed her comment to Angus and Cherry. 'That way none of us miss out. And Nat and Gabe will be over this afternoon too.'

'Good. It's a date!'

##

Sienna and Eliza went back to the day spa to meet the builders who were finalising the plumbing. Evie and Jed headed out to the gardens—Evie had allocated Jed to the ride-on mower and she was meeting with the new landscape gardener to show him around. Dylan had ticked all of Evie's boxes—and mine—he arrived today and was starting officially on Monday.

Rafe reached for my hand before he headed back to our house on the hill. He lifted my fingers to his lips. 'Happy?'

'Very.' I slipped my arms around his waist and inhaled that familiar aftershave. 'But I'm worried about you and that news you had.'

He nodded. 'I'm okay. I'm more worried about Odessa. I know how she can react when things go awry. I'm going to call her at the hospital.'

I frowned. 'But won't it be the middle of the night in England?'

He glanced at his watch. 'Almost midnight, but she'll still be awake.'

Exactly how well did Rafe know this Odessa? Another niggle of jealousy surfaced and I immediately felt guilty. The poor woman had been in an horrendous car accident where someone had died, and she was in hospital herself.

'You go and make your call, and I'll have this meeting with Tamsin and Angus.' I reached up and kissed him. 'I'll be back up for lunch.'

'I'll see you after.' Rafe looked past me and I knew his thoughts were already winging across the ocean.

Tamsin and Angus were sitting at a table at the back of the restaurant. The table was bare and someone had put a jug of water and three glasses on the table.

'Where's Cherry?' I asked.

'I didn't think we needed her for the meeting.' Angus' lips were set in a firm line.

'I like inclusivity here. And open communication. Tam and I will wait here while you go and get her.'

'Sure.' His nod was terse.

Tam waited until he was on the path and spoke softly. 'He didn't like that.'

'Well, he can learn to, or he can go. I'm not having personal issues or past histories impact on the operation of Ma Carmichael's.' I picked up the jug and poured water in each of the three glasses, and then walked over to the bar and got a fourth. 'How have you found them to be in the kitchen?'

'Workwise? They work really well together. Cherry knows exactly what he wants almost before he asks. Angus is a top-class chef, and he runs a good kitchen. I've stepped back the last week and worked with the builders in the new restaurant and kitchen. Renzo is fantastic; he's asked how I want every little thing.' She lowered her voice, and looked around but there was no one else in the building. 'A bit of gossip for you too, in case you haven't picked up on it. Danny Riccardo put himself in charge of the day spa, and Renzo was chuckling about it.'

'Why?'

'The attraction wasn't the building. It was Sienna. I've heard them chattering away in Italian quite a few times.'

'Ah, I see. He's not a bad looker and he's certainly built.'

'And Sienna's noticed that too, don't you worry.' Tam giggled. 'Another conquest for our love resort.'

We stopped giggling and sat up straight as we spotted Cherry coming along the path to the restaurant. Angus was about ten steps behind her, looking at the phone in his hand.

'Hi again. Take a seat, Cherry. I wanted you here so you're a part of the planning too.' I looked at Tam. 'I guess that's what you wanted to ask about?'

'Yes. We've got a few things to sort out.'

She paused as Angus came in and pulled out a chair and sat down. He put his phone face down on the table.

'The big question,' Tam said as she glanced at Angus, 'is whether we open the restaurant this week, or not.'

'I don't have a preference,' I replied.

Tam nodded. 'The old kitchen will still be operating the night of the wedding, but it will have a set menu to free Angus up to take over the reception catering. I've hired two chefs and Mirabelle for the guests next Saturday night, and then Angus and Cherry, a third casual chef, and two waitresses will work the wedding reception.'

'Sounds like it's all sorted. What did you need me for?' I asked.

Tam looked at Angus and back to me. 'There's two ways we can go. Do we have the wedding reception as the function that kicks it off, or do we serve the guests here before that?'

I shrugged. 'Like I said. Either way.'

'The issue is,' Angus interrupted, 'Tamsin would like to see your function as the first, but I'm in favour of at least a couple of trial runs with the guests. I'd hate to have an equipment failure or something that ruined your special night.'

I nodded and looked at Tam. 'That makes sense to me. Did you feel strongly about it?'

'No, but I thought you might like to "christen" the new restaurant by having your wedding as the first night.'

'Let's open it on Tuesday night. That should give you time to iron out any kinks, shouldn't it, Angus? I asked.

'Tuesday would be good.' He looked relieved and Cherry nodded.

'So, is there anything else?' I asked.

This time Angus smiled, and I thought how different he looked when he wasn't focused and serious. Or angry.

'I wanted to talk about the menu for the wedding, so I can get the order in.'

I looked at Tam, surprised she had handed that over to him, but she nodded and explained.

'Control freak that I am, I have totally handed the wedding planning, menus, and ordering to Angus. I'm a guest at this wedding, and I intend to enjoy every minute of it.'

'Excellent.' I turned to Angus. 'So what do you want to know?'

'I've got the canapes and entrees sorted, and I wanted to check the main with you. I'll offer a white meat alternative, but I have a great source for my beef, and I'd like to do a special steak with a variety of sauces as the main if you're happy with that.'

'That sounds good to me. It reminds me of that steak restaurant we loved down on the Gold Coast, remember it, Tam?'

'I do. AA's,' Tam said. 'They bought their beef from a property in Western Queensland and the sauces were divine. You didn't work there too, did you, Angus?'

Angus' smile disappeared as he let out a terse 'No,' and looked past me. Cherry lowered her gaze and her face was bright red. You could have cut the air with a knife. Tam and I looked at each other, wondering what was going on.

Chapter Fourteen

Cherry – Lord Howe Island

Cherry held her small purse tightly as she stepped out onto the veranda where Angus was waiting. He was wearing a pair of khaki chinos and an open-necked shirt.

'I hope I'm not overdressed. I didn't bring many clothes with me,' she said smoothing her hand down her dress nervously.

Angus' glance was admiring, and heat rose up her neck. What the hell was she doing going out with a guy on her first night on the island? And if she was honest, maybe it had been a mistake booking this holiday. She couldn't make up her mind.

'You look perfect.' His voice was a little bit husky and she looked down as he cleared his throat. 'Right to go?'

She nodded and he crooked his elbow. Cherry hesitated before she slipped her hand through, and was immediately conscious of his warm skin against her forearm.

Angus kept the conversation flowing as they walked the two hundred metres towards the lagoon. 'The restaurant is opposite the jetty just past Signal

Point.'

'You know the landmarks already,' Cherry
said quietly.

'I've examined the map of the whole island.
I loved my geography lessons at school,' he said
with a laugh. 'That and cooking were the only two
reasons to go to class. I wagged a lot, but it was
hard not to get caught at boarding school. Not many
places to hide.'

'I guess it would be.' Cherry thought back to
her school days. 'I loved school. I could lose myself
in my work. I hated leaving and not having that
structure in my life. I didn't know then what I
wanted to do.'

'My experience was a bit different. Look,
there it is.' Angus slowed and pointed to a building
on the beach side of the road. 'Hmmm, Trader
Bob's. It looks pretty ordinary, doesn't it?'

If she didn't know it was a restaurant it
could have passed as an old fishing shack. The
timber was faded and the guttering hung loose on
one side. But the view beyond was spectacular.

'Don't judge a book by its cover,' she said.
'It could be really good and you might decide you
have to work here.'

'Okay, let's go see. And please, not a word
about me being Angus Alexander. I hope you don't
mind, but I made the booking under your name and

your lodge. I don't want them to know I'm sussing them out.'

'That's fine, because I'm paying to thank you for your kindness today. I insist.'

'Okay, I'll accept if that's what you want, but on one condition.' His grin was cheeky.

'And what would that be?' she asked, still a little suspicious of his motive.

'I take you out tomorrow night, and *I* pay.'

Cherry laughed lightly as relief settled in her. 'Don't be too hasty. You'll probably find my company extremely boring, and you'll wish you hadn't said that. It would serve you right.'

'Nope, never,' he said as he stopped at the bottom of the steps leading to the restaurant. 'I find you fascinating, Cherry Chilcott. You're a mystery woman to me. So be warned. Tonight I will try to find out all your secrets.'

This time, Cherry's laugh was loud and she put her hand over her mouth when the couple waiting on the steps above them looked down at her. 'Sorry, Angus, I have no secrets at all. Unless failing sewing in Year 8 can be classed as a secret. Mrs Long hated me.'

'Ah ha,' he said triumphantly. 'See I've learned your first secret already.'

'You're mad,' she said unable to hold back another laugh.

'But loveable,' he said with a wink.

Cherry knew she was losing the battle to fight that rising tide of attraction every time Angus opened his mouth or looked at her.

##

Cherry enjoyed the night at Trader Bob's, and she enjoyed her meal despite Angus examining his main course with great attention and breaking it down into individual ingredients. They started off in the bar that overlooked the lagoon, and Angus ordered a beer for himself and the red wine she requested when he asked.

They sat back in the dated eighties cane chairs and he pulled a face at the tired fishing nets and plastic fish draped behind the bar.

'Could do with a revamp.'

'You're not impressed yet, are you?' she asked quietly when the barman moved slowly along the bar to serve the only other couple in the restaurant. 'But remember, guests come for the food, not the decor.'

'I'll tell you when we eat,' he whispered back. 'It doesn't seem to be busy.'

'It's only early.'

'We'll see.'

By the time they were shown to their table

in the corner overlooking the lagoon, Angus seemed
to relax a bit. 'Good view. That's a plus.'

'And look,' Cherry said as she saw the
island bus pull up outside and a dozen or so couples
got off. 'It's very popular.'

'Or it could be Ronny's advertising.'
Despite his negative words, Angus' grin was wide.

The waitress—an older woman with grey
hair—came out of the kitchen with an order pad in
hand. 'Good evening, Mr and Mrs Chilcott, I'm
Delores, and I'm your waitress for tonight. I'd
suggest you order now, or it might be a long wait
for your dinner.' She gestured with her head to the
group who were coming up the outside stairs. Her
pencil was poised and she waited, staring at Angus.

'That's fine, we're not in a rush, are we, Mrs
Chilcott?' His eyes danced as he observed Cherry,
and she played along.

'No, Mr Chilcott, I'm happy to linger over
dinner.'

Delores shrugged and tucked the pencil in
her hair above her ear. 'Okay, I'll come back and
take your orders in a while then.'

Cherry held up her hand as she went to walk
away. 'Ah, could we see a menu so we can decide
what we want?'

'Didn't Bob give you one at the bar?'
'No,' Cherry said.

Delores rolled her eyes but was soon back with two photocopied sheets.

Angus stared at her, and then at the photocopied menus, before turning back to look at the bar. She felt sorry for him as a look of despair shadowed his eyes.

Cherry reached out and put her hand on his arm. 'Just think how disappointed you would have been if you'd accepted the job without coming over first.'

He pulled a face. '*And* if I'd signed up for two years.'

'But we might be judging too quickly. Wait until your meal arrives. It might be incredible.'

Angus picked up the photocopied menus and read the selection to her. His words were delivered in a monotone, but a smile crept onto his face.

'Kingfish with salad. Kingfish with mashed potato. Kingfish with roast potatoes.' His voice went husky again as he chuckled and a shiver ran up her back. Cherry found it hard to take her eyes off him.

'Island beef with salad. Island beef with mashed potatoes. Island beef with roast potatoes.' He was grinning so much, he could barely get the last two words out.

She smiled back. He made her feel comfortable, and relaxed and sympathetic and she cared what he thought about her.

'I was hoping for a chicken dish,' she said.

Angus snorted and Cherry lifted her napkin and put it to her mouth.

'Chicken with salad, chicken with mashed—'

'Stop it,' she said as she giggled behind the napkin.

'So what are you going to choose?'

'You're the chef. What would you recommend?'

'Definitely the kingfish.'

'Okay. Kingfish it is.'

'Let's begin with the mixed entrée. It's a platter of island produce.'

Cherry kept her face straight. 'Kingfish?'

'We'll find out.'

Before Delores came back for their order, Angus looked over at the bar. 'Would you like to share a bottle of wine with me?'

'As long as it's white wine to go with my kingfish,' she replied demurely.

'Not your usual red?'

'Ugh. Not with fish.'

'White wine it is then.' He stood and went over to the bar, and Cherry took the opportunity to study Angus. The khaki chinos moulded his thighs snugly and it sent a quiver spiking into her lower belly. She hadn't experienced that desire for a long time.

'Stop it,' she told herself.

She looked down when he came back with a bottle of wine and two glasses. The last thing she wanted was for him to see her staring at him.

'Surprisingly they had some good whites to choose from. I hope this one is okay.' Angus held up the bottle with a Hunter Valley label.

'That's fine.'

After their orders were placed, and they waited for their meals, he put one elbow on the table and propped his chin in his hand. 'Thank you for coming with me tonight. I don't think I could have lasted the distance by myself. I would have walked out by now.'

Cherry wagged her finger at him. 'You've made an assumption about the food, and you might be wrong, you know.'

'I doubt it.'

Five minutes later, Angus was eating the mixed entrée *and* eating his words.

Cherry couldn't help the giggle that bubbled up, and the second glass of wine had relaxed her even more.

He put some beef onto his fork, and dipped into the bowl of wasabi on the side, and took a bite. His eyes widened. She watched intently as he did it again.

And again.

Finally he looked up. 'That is superb. I take back every assumption I made tonight.'

'So are you going to'—she lowered her voice—'reconsider the job offer?'

'I think I'll wait for the main and the dessert.' Angus held her eyes with his and Cherry couldn't look away. 'What do you think?' he asked.

She looked around at the restaurant. 'I don't think it suits you. The restaurant and the small island.'

'You've picked me well. You're spot on.'

There was silence for a while as they both cleared their plates. After Delores appeared and took the plates away, Angus lifted the bottle and raised his eyebrows, and Cherry was surprised to see her glass was empty.

She nodded.

When he'd half-filled her glass with wine, she sat back and looked at him again. Two glasses of wine had given her courage.

'You've talked about me and my secrets. Tell me about Angus Alexander and what he really wants, because I know it's not this.'

'What do I want? You realise that if I tell you, I'll have to lock you away in my dungeon before you accidentally spread the word.'

'What word would that be?' Cherry asked before taking another sip.

'Seriously? My dream?'

She nodded again.

'It's my dream to own an exclusive restaurant where I can source my beef from my family cattle property. Cook a variety of beef dishes with some of the sauces I've created over the past few years.' He lowered his voice. 'It might sound as though I'm up myself, Cherry, but I'm very good at what I do. But before that I need a job where I can fly. A job that will let me earn enough money to start my own place.'

'That sounds like a worthwhile dream.'

Not like me, she thought. Lurching from one job to another, knowing what she wanted to do, but not having the courage to do it. She shook herself mentally, and put her head to the side.

'What would you call this place of yours?'

'Might sound a bit simple and silly, but I've had the idea for a long time. I've designed the logo for the restaurant, the black serviettes and the layout.'

'So what will it be called. *When* you do it, not *if*.'

'Simply AA's. Do you think that sounds silly or okay? It's always been in my mind.'

'Because it's your initials?'

'No.' He shook his head. 'That's a coincidence. It's the brand we use on our cattle. Dad's property—or the family property, it's fourth generation—is called Linden Downs, but we've used AA for our cattle since the early days.'

'A great family history.' She tipped her head to the side and looked at him curiously. 'It's a big move from a cattle station to the Gold Coast, but even more to a tiny island in the middle of the ocean. How come you didn't stay on the property.'

He stared past her and Cherry wondered if she was getting too personal.

'It wasn't the life I wanted, and I didn't get on with the old man. He has no respect for my choice of career, and I guess my motivation for AA's comes from wanting to prove myself to him.'

'Is it worth the angst? Will it really make a difference?'

'You sound like you're talking from personal experience.'

She lifted her head and lost herself in Angus' steady gaze only half aware of the waitress delivering the main course.. 'My lack of self-confidence, and my lack of settling into a career that I want comes from my father's constant reminder that I don't measure up to my brother and sister. I'm smart enough to know why I feel that way, but I can never get the self-confidence to do something about it.'

'I'm sorry to hear that. Parents can sure mess us up, can't they?'

Cherry pulled back. The conversation was getting a bit serious and she'd let out more about herself than she'd ever done before. With a nod, she looked up at the menu board that was up behind the bar. 'That fish was excellent, how about some dessert to soak up all this wine before I tell you all my secrets?

A slow, sexy smile spread across his face. 'There's more?'

That damn quiver tugged at her again, and she couldn't help flirting back. 'Could be.'

'Tell me the first one then. Your favourite dessert.'

Cherry answered immediately. 'That's easy. Pavlova and fresh fruit.'

Angus shook his head. 'I'll have to educate you in the delights of what I can do with chocolate.'

Heat rushed up her face as her imagination ran wild, but she smiled. 'So what will you choose off the dessert menu?'

Sexual tension hummed around them. He looked at her for a long time before he answered. 'I'll surprise you.'

The mood intensified as they shared two dessert plates—Angus' surprise *was* chocolate mousse—and finished the wine. Cherry pulled her purse out to retrieve her credit card, but Angus shook his head. 'It's already paid for. It was a set price including the wine, so I fixed it up at the bar.' He held up his hand. 'Your shout tomorrow night, if you insist.'

It was natural for Cherry to slip her hand though his arm as they walked down the steps. When they reached the turn to Lagoon Road that led to their lodges, Angus paused. 'How about a walk on the beach? The moonrise isn't far off.'

As they stepped onto the sand the sky to the east began to glow, and the ragged clouds above the horizon were edged with silver. A path of light began at the horizon and slowly crept across the still waters of the lagoon as moonrise approached.

There was no hesitation when Angus paused and looked down at her. He cupped his hands on her cheeks and Cherry opened her lips slightly as he pressed his mouth against hers.

The sensation of his lips sliding gently against hers set butterflies fluttering in her belly. She pressed her hand against his chest and pulled her head back a little bit.

'I'm sorry,' he said. 'I should have asked first.'

Cherry drew a quick breath and made a decision. 'No, there was no need to ask.' She stood

on her toes and lifted her lips to meet his. This time
there was no pulling away.

Chapter Fifteen

Angus -Lord Howe Island

Angus Alexander was in love. He had been since he'd first spotted Cherry at the airport. He just had to convince her it was the real thing, and not a holiday fling. Three days had passed since the first night when he had kissed her as they watched the moon rise on the beach. They'd sat there on the sand together until the moon was high in the sky, and talked and kissed and then talked some more. Cherry had nestled against him as they'd walked back to the lodges after midnight.

He knew she was wary, and he was going to have to work hard to convince her that he really wanted to see her when they got back to the Gold Coast. He'd take the job at Surfside. Even though he'd been unexpectedly surprised by the quality of the food at Trader Bob's, it wasn't the type of restaurant he wanted to work at. And the island was not where he wanted to live.

He knew if he was willing, there would be overtime at Surfside, and he would save as hard as he could. He'd give it a year or two, and then see if he was in a position to start up his own place. He could start small and exclusive.

A tap on the door pulled him from his

thoughts and he smiled.

'Are you ready?' Cherry stood there, and the sight of her in skin-tight walking pants and a singlet top made his mouth dry.

Angus swallowed. 'Sure am.'

Cherry was still shy with him, and displayed a lack of confidence he hadn't seen before. He opened his arms in invitation and she stepped in, lifting her face for a good morning kiss.

'Sleep well?' he asked.

'I did. I'm full of energy and ready for this trek.'

Angus was full of energy, but his thoughts headed in a different direction than the climb they had planned up Malabar Hill. He let her go and reached for the backpack he'd filled with some snacks he'd bought at the store yesterday afternoon.

Cherry pointed to her pack. 'I've got water, and the kitchen at the lodge made some sandwiches for us.'

'Great, we're set, let's go.'

He held out his hand and Cherry slipped hers into it as they set off down the road towards Ned's Beach where the Malabar track started.

'I used the internet computer at the General Store when I went down last night,' he said as they stepped into the forest.

She raised her eyebrows in question.

'I accepted the position at Surfside. Not as high a position as I'd hoped for, but it will be more experience for me.' He squeezed her fingers lightly.

'That's good. That is, if that's what you wanted.' Colour stained her cheekbones, and she looked down. Angus held back the questions he wanted to ask her. Why was she so shy, and why did she hesitate each time she asked him something? It was almost as though she sought approval for everything she said, and did, and considered her actions and words before she spoke. Someone had really done a number on her.

'And it means I'll be able to see a lot more of you,' he said. He stopped walking and looked down at her. 'I mean it, Cherry. It's not a holiday fling. I know it's only been a few days, but I'd like to think we can go somewhere with this.'

Angus was surprised when she put her pack on the ground, and lifted her arms to go around his neck. 'I hope so. That would be really good.'

Her lips were soft and warm, and for a moment he considered cancelling the walk and inviting her back to his room, but he didn't want to rush her. They had all the time in the world.

***

The five days on Lord Howe Island had wrought a change in Cherry. It had taken time, but she'd finally relaxed in Angus' company. She trusted him and was looking forward to seeing him when they got back home.

She looked around the room, and when she was satisfied she hadn't missed anything, zipped her suitcase shut before wheeling it out onto the porch.

The last five days had been incredible; Cherry had pushed her boundaries and taken risks. Not only in physical activities but personally, in being able to trust. She and Angus had spent every daylight hour together; they'd snorkelled, and climbed Malabar Hill, and trekked down to Old Gulch, and Angus had complained as they'd had to walk back up the seven hundred steps.

'You're a sook,' she'd teased him, and he'd grabbed her and kissed her until she stopped laughing at him.

Every evening they tried a different restaurant, and then walked home along the beach. Each outing had brought them closer, and they'd walked and talked nonstop. Angus had told her about growing up in the Gulf country on the family cattle property, and Cherry had shared a little about her childhood. Just touched on it briefly with a joke and a laugh; she knew deep down how much it had scarred her, but didn't want to be negative.

The day they'd snorkelled in the lagoon, Angus had stayed by her side and made sure she was okay the whole time they were in the water. She'd felt cherished for the first time in her life.

They'd had breakfast at the coffee shop near the lagoon this morning, before they walked back to the lodges to pack for the afternoon flight home.

'Do you think you'd come back here with me one day?' he asked quietly as they sat looking at the water.

'We didn't have time to do everything in the end, did we?' she replied.

'I was thinking more about the great memories it's made for us.'

'That's a sweet thing to say.'

Angus reached across the table and took her hand. 'I'm very grateful that we were given seats together on the flight over.'

'Me too. Even though I made a fool of myself.'

'How are you feeling about flying back?' His thumb brushed the skin on the back of her hand and that familiar quiver tugged low in her belly again.

'I'm fine,' she said with a smile. Cherry had been so immersed in her thoughts of Angus, and the wonderful time she'd had on the island she hadn't had time to get nervous about the flight home.

And she *was* fine.

The flight home was uneventful, the weather was calm and they landed in Brisbane without incident. Uneventful, that was, in terms of the air travel, but Cherry found it hard to ignore the feelings that ran rampant through her, every time their hands or legs touched on the flight. The sexual tension had been building all week, but they'd taken it no further than kissing.

'How were you planning on getting home from the airport?' Angus asked as he lifted her suitcase off the baggage carousel. 'Do you have a car at the airport?'

'No. I don't own a car. I'll catch the airport train to Southport and then pick up the light rail to my apartment. There's a stop about a hundred metres away.'

'How about I give you a lift? I go through Southport on my way home. My car's in the long term parking here. It'd be much quicker for you, and I'd love the company.'

'That would be great. Thank you, I accept.'

The drive down to the coast was broken intermittently by short conversations about work; it was as though Angus had switched out of holiday mode.

And Cherry mode.

His aftershave wafted over her, and Cherry knew she couldn't let him go without . . .

Without what?

Without trying.

What was the right thing to say?

Would you like to come inside and kiss me?

Should she invite him in for coffee? Or a drink? It was that time of day.

Or would he want to drop her off and head straight back to his pre-holiday life? Had she read too much into their time together? A light holiday romance, it sure couldn't be called a fling.

Maybe he already had plans.

Or was she reading too much into what he'd said? Maybe the offer of a lift to the coast was him being polite. She couldn't help letting out a small sigh and Angus glanced over at her.

'Tired?'

'A little. Back to reality.'

As they turned off the Motorway, Cherry directed him. 'I'm in Parker Street just off Marine Parade. Halfway along on the left.'

There was a car parking space outside the apartment block, and Angus walked around to the back of his SUV and took her suitcase out.

'Well,' he said, 'I guess—'

'Would you like to come in?' Cherry blurted

out. 'Um for a coffee, or a drink, or—'

Angus looked at her without speaking, but picked up her suitcase and followed her to the lift.

Not a word was spoken as it took them to the third floor, and the silence was laden with tension.

***

Angus was close behind Cherry and he noticed her hand was shaking as she put the key in her door and pushed it open. When he followed her in, she turned to look at him, her eyes wide, not speaking, but she didn't move away. He put the suitcase down and with a groan, pulled her hard against him.

When she reached up and grabbed his hair and leaned into him, Cherry's lips were only a breath away. He lowered his head, and her mouth opened beneath his, her hands slipping beneath his T-shirt. Desire overwhelmed him and he deepened the kiss, wanting, needing his mouth on hers.

'You are the most beautiful woman I have ever known,' he murmured. 'You know I'm falling in love with you, don't you?'

'I've never felt this way before,' she said against his mouth, her voice low and husky. A spark sizzled between them and he could feel her heart pounding against his chest. 'I just couldn't let you leave.'

'I didn't want to leave you,' he replied.

'Do you need to get home?' She leaned against him for a moment and then lifted her head and smiled up at him. 'Or maybe . . .'

'Maybe?'

'Maybe . . . would you like to stay the night?'

Angus pulled her close to him and his answer was in his kiss.

Chapter Sixteen

Cherry – Gold Coast – six months later

'What shift are you on tonight?' Angus called from the bathroom as he stepped out of the shower in Cherry's apartment. The towel rail squeaked as he pulled the towel off it.

Cherry glanced up at the clock. 'Early shift,' she called back. 'You'd better hurry, or you're going to be late.' Angus had spent the night at her apartment, as he did more often than not these days.

The week after they'd come back from Lord Howe Island, Angus had started his new job at Surfside at Broadwater, and he'd been disappointed when Cherry had transferred to the Surfside hotel located at Surfers Paradise.

She'd told him that it was better that they didn't work at the same hotel. 'I don't want you to get sick of me, seeing me every day and night,' she said.

'No fear of that happening, sweetheart,' he'd replied.

The truth was Cherry didn't want Angus to see her at work. She found it hard enough to put on the fun personality, and be loud and vivacious as she mixed the cocktails and sang to the customers.

She'd be mortified if Angus saw her putting on her act. She glanced down at her bag where she'd placed her uniform when he was in the shower.

The time they spent together was wonderful, but she wanted to keep her job out of it. She couldn't even explain to herself why she felt like that; she just knew it was better if he knew the real Cherry, not the person she had to be when she sang for strangers.

Angus hurried out of the bathroom, buttoning up his white shirt. 'I've got a split shift. Lunch and then back to prep for dinner. We've got a function, so I'll be late too.' He came across to the table where Cherry was sipping her second coffee of the morning. 'Do you want me to go home to my place or come here?' He dropped a quick kiss on the top of her head. 'You know, it's about time we thought about getting a place together. We wouldn't have to juggle seeing each other around our shifts.'

Cherry hesitated. 'We'll talk about it when you have more time. Now get out of here or you won't have a job.'

'I'm going. Okay, we'll talk later and I've got some news for you. A surprise.'

She smiled when he came back from the door and kissed her again. 'Tell me now, you know I hate surprises.'

'I think I've found a building for me to start

up my own place. Do you think Robina is too far away from town to start up AA's - From Paddock to Plate?' The pride in Angus' voice when he talked about his plans made her smile even more. He was so excited about his project.

'Tell me more tonight. And yes, come back here. I'll be home about eleven.'

He kissed her again before he hurried across to the door. 'Have a good day, babe.'

She blew him a kiss as the door closed behind him.

Life was good; she never thought she could be so happy.

***

Angus closed the door of the cool room with a hard shove and carried the steaks to the countertop. He was seething; his nemesis, Alan Garner, had been waiting in the car park for him when he'd arrived at work.

'G'day, Angus.' Garner's usual slimy smile accompanied his words.

'Can't talk, sorry. I'm running late.'

'Okay. I'll be quick. I've got a job offer for you.'

Angus paused and kept his tone polite. 'I've got a job I'm happy with, but thanks anyway.'

'Mine's better.' Garner's smile widened. 'It's an opportunity you can't pass up, mate. I'm starting up a small exclusive steak restaurant in Labrador.' He stared at Angus. 'Getting my beef from a top property in the central west. "From Paddock to Plate", my slogan will be. I've already got an interview on a TV morning show next week. There's lots of media interest. A great opportunity for you to improve your skills and get yourself a profile.'

'Are you taking the piss out of me?' Angus stared at him in disbelief. 'What did you say it was called?'

'AA's.' Garner pushed himself away from the car bonnet he was leaning on and puffed his chest out. 'You got a problem with that?'

'Bloody oath, I have.'

'Trademarked it, have you?'

Angus swallowed down his anger, but his voice rose. 'No, but it's from my family property. You've stolen my idea. Who told you what I was doing?'

'Mate, I have no idea what you're talking about. "AA's" comes from Angus Downs where I'll be sourcing my beef. It's my concept, and it's underway. I'm ready to start hiring. So are you interested? You could learn a lot from me.'

Angus stared at him. 'Fuck off, Garner.' He

turned on his heel and strode to the back door of the kitchen.

The day was long, and a mother of a headache was pounding at his temples by the time the main course had gone out to the function room. He headed to the small bathroom at the back of the staffroom and popped two paracetamol.

How the hell had Garner heard about his plans? He'd never talked about it at any of his workplaces. Surely it wasn't a coincidence?

No, it couldn't be. The name, the slogan and the concept. The bastard had somehow got wind of it and stolen his idea. The look on Garner's face had been a dead giveaway. They'd been playing a game of one-upmanship for years.

And for the bastard to have the bloody hide to offer him a job, so he could learn something from him. The anger roiled in Angus' gut and he felt like spewing.

How the hell had he got all that information?

It couldn't have been Cherry. She was the only one he'd told.

Surely not.

The kitchen was quiet when he went back in. The head chef called him over. 'We're all set for dessert, because they've got a massive cake out there. Seeing you did the split shift, you can knock off now if you like, Angus.'

'Thanks, Joe, I will.' Angus looked up at the clock. It was only eight-thirty.

He needed a drink—once the headache eased— and he need a sympathetic ear. He'd get changed and head over to see Cherry at the bar in Surfers. He'd never been there, because they tried to work the same nights so they could have time off together.

Bloody hell. The hide of that slime bag, and the worst thing was, if Garner was telling the truth, there was nothing Angus could do about it.

***

Being a Saturday night, the bar where Cherry worked was packed, and the requests for fancy cocktails and special song requests came thick and fast. There were four of them working the bar tonight, and when the mike pinned to her low-cut T-shirt slipped, Cherry repinned it. As she looked up, she noticed a guy at the end of the bar, his gaze stuck on her breasts. She gritted her teeth and turned her back on him. The uniform for the girls behind the bar was one she didn't like; Mike, the new manager had insisted on the shorts and the tight T-shirts the day he'd taken over. She couldn't say anything because business had really picked up, as had her tips. But the clothes made her

162

uncomfortable, so uncomfortable that she never hung them on the line when Angus was staying, nor did she get dressed in the apartment.

It was time to start looking for another job.

Maybe if Angus got his restaurant up and running she could waitress there. Maybe he'd even be receptive to taking her on as a trainee chef. She pulled a face as she turned back to serve the patrons queued at the bar. She'd never told him what her dream was; he thought she was happy doing the casual work that paid the bills.

Over the years of casual work, she'd saved a significant nest egg, and this weekend she was going to sit Angus down and see if he'd let her invest in his restaurant.

'Two more minutes, Chezza, and I'll switch the sound system back on. Once this crowd clears,' Mike yelled as he walked past.

'That's not my name,' Cherry felt like snapping, but as usual, she put her head down and nodded. Her self-confidence had built a little since she'd been with Angus, six months of happiness had made her feel good about herself, but she still wasn't strong enough to stand up to Mike.

The next order came in. 'A Mata Hari and *Kokomo*, please, gorgeous.'

Cherry plastered a smile on her face, switched the mike on, picked up the cocktail shaker, and segued into work mode.

'Aruba, Jamaica . . .' Her voice was clear and the patrons queued at the bar quietened as the song filled the air.

When she'd finished, the guy at the end of the bar gestured for her to come over. She looked around hoping one of the other attendants was free, but they all had a three-deep queue in front of them. Reluctantly she walked to the end of the bar; you could pick a difficult patron from a mile off and this one had sleazeball written all over him.

'What can I get you, sir?' she asked resisting the effort to pull up the neckline of her T-shirt as his gaze settled on her breasts. 'Another cocktail, or a beer?' She took the empty glass from the countertop in front of him.

'No, darlin'. I'll have another one of your fancy cocktails please, and a sexy song to go with it.'

Yep, she'd picked him all right.

'What would you like?' She stood back but he spoke so quietly she couldn't hear his order over the noise in the bar. He winked at her and waited.

'I'm sorry I didn't catch your order, sir.'

'I'll have a Climax please, sweetheart.' His grin was as sleazy as the rest of him and Cherry resisted rolling her eyes.

'Would you prefer that with Amaretto or

Frangelico, sir?'

'You choose, darlin'. Have one with me'—he winked—'and put it on my tab.'

'No, thank you. We don't drink on duty.' Cherry leaned forward to make sure he heard her, and he grabbed her arm. He held it so tightly she couldn't pull away. Leaning forward he was almost nose to nose with her.

'I didn't tell you my song.'

'Okay, what song are you requesting?' She tried to pull back but his grip was like iron. She flicked a glance up the bar but everyone was busy and there was no sign of Mike.

'Erotic City. The Prince song. Do you know it, babe?'

'No, I'm sorry, I don't.'

'Well, babe, you pick a sexy one just for me.' His face was so close his beer breath brushed her cheek and she gritted her teeth. 'Maybe we'll have that drink when you knock off.'

'Let me go, so I can make your cocktail, sir.'

He shook his head and his grip tightened. Flicking his eyes down to the front of her T-shirt, he shook his head slowly. 'Nope, I'm enjoying the view right where I am.'

She tensed in his grip. 'Let go of me, *now*.'

'Cherry, can you get back to work and stop talking to the customers please.' She was relieved to hear Mike, the manager, behind her. He must have seen she was being hassled.

Her arm was released and she moved back quickly. 'Amaretto, it is.'

She quickly made the cocktail without her usual flourish, and she didn't sing as she made it.

Mike called her over after the crowd had cleared from the bar. 'A word please, Cherry.'

She held her hair back with one hand and then wiped the perspiration off her brow with the other. 'Yes?'

'In future keep your flirting for out of hours, please, or I'll dock your pay.'

'What?' Shock jarred through her. 'Flirting? Me?'

'You looked like you were really getting it on with that guy. It's not a good look.'

'Mike, he was coming onto me. I don't even know him. He had hold of my arm and I couldn't pull away.'

'That's not what it looked like from where I was standing. Consider this a first warning.'

'It was almost assault.' She bit her lip as she stared up at him but he turned away.

'Cut the excuses and get singing, or I will dock you.'

Cherry stood there after he walked away. Disbelief rattled her. The injustice of his comment and his warning rankled, and she wished she'd had the confidence to stand up for herself, and force him to listen to her.

She wished she'd stood up to both of them. Her boss and the sleazeball.

Her ears buzzed as the noise of the bar faded around her, and stared at the crowd calling to get the bar attendants' attention.

I hate this job. She hated the falseness, she hated the songs she had to sing, and she hated her uniform. She'd gone along with it all for long enough. It was not what she wanted to do; it was time to chase her dream, and try to get work in the food side of hospitality. She'd given up, not having faith in herself.

It was time.

Taking a deep breath, Cherry walked across to Mike's office behind the bar, ignoring the song requests that were yelled at her as she walked through the bar.

'What's wrong now?' he said tersely.

'Nothing,' she said sweetly. 'I've had enough. I'm leaving.'

'What? When?' Panic crossed his face and she knew that he didn't want to lose his singing waitress. He'd been bullying her.

'Now. Take my notice out of whatever pay you owe me. I've had enough.'

Walking out of the bar was one of the most satisfying things Cherry had ever done. She went to the staffroom, collected her bag and walked out without a backward glance. Satisfaction that she'd finally stood up for herself and put her notice in filled her with pride. It was well overdue.

Wait until she told Angus. With a smile she headed for the light rail station.

Chapter Seventeen

Cherry -Pentecost Island

Working in close proximity to Angus in the small space of the kitchen in the original house on Pentecost Island was doing Cherry's head in. Not that there had been any harsh words or unreasonable behaviour. After their spectacular initial blow-up in front of Pippa and Tamsin, they had been unfailingly polite to each other. She was still embarrassed about that blow-up and she couldn't even remember what was said.

Requests like "Pass the frypan, plate up, please, and more sauce" had been the sum total of their interactions for over a week. The tension waiting for him to break had been unbearable, and she was on edge every minute she was in the kitchen with him.

She stifled a yawn as she wiped down the last benchtop. The prep had been done for tonight's meals, and Angus had left to go down to Pippa's sunset drinks thing on the beach.

The drinks that were celebrating the completion of the day spa, and the move to the new restaurant and kitchen. She was supposed to go down when she finished, but the respite from

Angus' company would be better than socialising. He'd filled her dreams at night—when she'd managed to get to sleep, and she'd been in the kitchen with him from morning until late. Even though it had been fitted out with new equipment, there was stuff to move over and that had been Angus' parting words to her before he'd gone to get changed.

'Please meet me here tomorrow at eight a.m. sharp. Tam wants us both to help her move to the new kitchen.'

'I will.' She'd lowered her eyes as she'd spoken, because it still hurt too much to look at him. It was almost eighteen months since he'd left her, the night he'd been going to come home and talk over his new venture with her and he'd never arrived. The night she'd quit her job.

She'd come home from the bar that night, to an empty apartment, and had waited up for him until after midnight. Eventually, she'd gone to bed, and hadn't worried; Angus sometimes got caught up and if it was too late, he'd go home to his own place.

She'd begun to worry the following afternoon. They'd never gone more than half a day without a call or a text to touch base.

Something had held her back from calling him—her old lack of confidence kicked in, or maybe it had been a premonition.

When will I see u?

No, she'd deleted that and started again.

Everything okay?

And then deleted that.

Cross at herself, her fingers flew over the keys. For goodness sake, they'd been seeing each other for almost six months.

Hi there. I'm going grocery shopping soon. Will u be here for dinner or did u pick up an extra shift? Love u x

When no answer had come by that night she really began to worry. Maybe Angus had been in an accident. Maybe he'd been hurt.

The next morning, she jumped on the light rail, and headed over to his apartment. Even if he was working extra shifts, he'd been there until eleven. Relief flooded though her when she spotted his car under the awning at the front of the apartment block. She buzzed his apartment and stood waiting for the door to open.

But it had stayed firmly shut.

She pulled out her phone and texted him.

I'm downstairs.

There was no answer. Finally, she turned away, not sure what to do next.

As she walked down the path the main door of the apartment block opened and she turned.

Angus stood there, and Cherry put her hand to her chest as sweet relief flooded in.

'Thank goodness,' she said. As she got closer, her eyes raked his set face. Dark shadows circled his eyes, and he didn't smile as she approached. 'Angus, what's wrong? Are you sick?'

'No. I'm fine.' He stood at the door and held it half-closed behind him. His expression didn't change as he stared at her as if he didn't know her. As if he hadn't ever loved her, and been the source of her happiness and contentment for half a year.

Panic began to build in Cherry's chest, and she put one hand out. 'What . . .what's the matter?'

'We're done, Cherry. If there's anything of mine at your place, just chuck it. I won't be coming to get it.'

'What do you mean, done?'

'I can't make myself any clearer. We're done. Finished. Over. Kaput.'

Cherry's throat ached as she tried to swallow. Tears stung her eyes. 'I don't understand.'

Angus stepped inside the door and before he closed it, his voice was hard. 'If there is one thing I won't tolerate it's dishonesty. You broke my trust.'

The door shut and he was gone.

She stood there, her heart pounding and thought about ringing him and insisting that he come down and tell her what he was on about.

Dishonesty? Trust? What was she supposed to have done?

She'd done nothing and he was simply making it up so he could break it off with her. Rage seethed through her. The last six months had been a total sham.

Men. She was over them. In the whole of her twenty-five and a half years she'd never met one she could trust. Or respect.

That was it. She was done; she'd move away and chase her dream.

As far away from Angus and her family as she could get.

##

Two weeks later, when Cherry locked up her apartment, handed the key in, her self-confidence had plummeted to rock bottom. Deep in her heart, she'd held onto a small hope that Angus would call and say it was all a mistake. Not once in the six months they'd been together had he ever shown any temper or any of that icy coldness that she'd seen on that last afternoon. A couple of times she'd been very close to going over to see him, but had thought better of it.

The phone call home to tell her family she was moving to North Queensland was almost as bad as Angus' betrayal, but she was able to let that go.

She'd always known she was worth nothing to her father, but she'd believed that Angus had loved her.

'Cherry?' Tamsin's call made her jump and she swung around, the damp cloth falling to the floor.

'I just came to see how much longer you'd be.' Tamsin walked over, a frown marring her pretty face. 'What's wrong?

Cherry lifted a hand to her face; she hadn't realised that tears had fallen while she was thinking back to how much Angus had hurt her.

'Has Angus been giving you a hard time?'

She shook her head. 'No. No, not at all. He's been fine.'

Tamsin came over and took her arm. 'Would it help to talk about it?'

Cherry shook her head again. 'There's nothing to talk about.'

'Well, come on, I'll wait while you get changed.'

'I might give it a miss.'

'You can't. It's extra important that you're there.'

'Why?

'You'll see. Pippa has an announcement to make.' Tamsin chuckled. 'If you hadn't noticed, she loves the limelight. She's a drama queen. But we all love her.' Her grin widened. 'Between you and me I might go one up on her tonight. Come on. I want you down there too.'

Cherry smiled through her tears, and then brushed the back of her hand over her eyes. 'Okay, give me five.'

She hurried into her small room at the back of the house, pulled a dress over her head, and came back via the bathroom where she scrubbed her face, and put on some lipstick. She pinched her cheeks, slipped the scrunchie off and let her hair hang loose before she met Tamsin on the veranda.

'I wish I could do that,' Tamsin said as they walked towards the beach together.

'Do what?'

'Make myself look that good in five minutes. You look gorgeous, Cherry, and I love that dress.'

'Thank you. And I love the vintage look you wear. And don't worry, you already look good. You have the most beautiful skin. You're glowing tonight.'

'I'm happy,' Tamsin said simply. 'Very happy.'

It only took a minute before they reached the beach, and Cherry was surprised to see how many people were there.

Tamsin paused as they stepped onto the sand, and Cherry slowed to wait for her.

'It's hard to believe how far we've come in less than a year, you know. This time a year ago, it was Pippa, Nell and I sitting on that beach, with Pippa looking daggers up the hill at Rafe. Now look at us. A week out from their wedding, and a resort almost built. There's been lots of changes and there are more on the way.'

Cherry looked across at the group as Gabe left and walked across to Tamsin. There were about thirty people gathered on the sand around a fold-up table that held bottles of champagne and glasses. Everyone looked happy and the mood was bright, and the conversations were buzzing. She kept her gaze from Angus. She'd seen enough of him this week already, and her job description did not include socialising with the sous chef.

'Come on, Cherry, I'll get you both a drink,' Gabe offered.

'Even though I'm working in an hour?' Cherry asked.

'Yes, it's a celebration,' Tam said.' And it might make it a bit easier for you working in that tense kitchen. I've been worried about how it's going.' Tamsin's glance settled on Angus before she switched it back to Cherry. 'Go over and join the girls.'

She walked across the sand and stood at the edge of the group. Tess was holding court and giggling as she talked. She looked up and spotted Cherry.

'Hey, Cherry. Do you remember Priscilla from Hamo? The woman who lived in the apartment under ours.'

Cherry had shared an apartment with Tess when she'd first arrived on Hamilton Island. It had been a surprise to bump into Tess her first week there. 'The one you called Prissy because she was always so proper.' She nodded her thanks when Tam walked over and handed her a glass of champagne. 'And she had that precious cat.'

'That's the one. She always carried on about being a vegan, and she was so perfect. That cultured voice and no swearing . . . ever! And I had no problem with that, but . . .' Tess giggled again and Cherry wondered how many glasses of bubbles she'd had. 'I was sitting on the balcony last week and she had a couple of friends over and I was surprised when this wonderful aroma of meat lovers pizza drifted up to me.'

'Wouldn't have been hers,' Cherry said. 'I endured a few food lectures from Prissy about food when she found out I worked in hospitality. She lectured me: "I have nothing to do with any products derived wholly or partly from animals." Geez, she used to bail me up every time I headed to work.'

'You'll love this! She's a fraud, Cherry. I was on my balcony last Saturday and all of a sudden there's this screeching and all I could hear was Prissy yelling out and swearing her head off. She kept yelling out, "you little bitch" and I wondered what on earth was happening. She *never* swore! I leaned over the balcony and her precious cat was on the table sitting in the middle of the huge pizza, and eating the salami.'

Tess let out a cackle and Mirabelle—who'd lived with them for a while—joined in with her snorting laugh.

'And then she yelled out, "That was my pizza, you little bitch."' Tess was shaking with laugher. 'Oh, you should have seen it. I've seen her a couple of times since and she won't look at me now.'

Cherry started to chuckle as she imagined the perfectly prissy Priscilla doing that. Just went to show you, she thought, people can put on an act. Speaking of which she stared across the beach at Angus who was standing on the edge of a group, and actually looking quite uncomfortable.

Good! she thought. About time he learned a lesson. Laughing at Tess's story had relaxed her and she sipped at her glass of champagne. For the past few days, Cherry had been wondering if she could do this, but by God, she could and she would.

Whatever the problem was, it was Angus' issue and not hers.

She had been thinking about pulling the pin and going back to Hamo to do casual waitressing but stuff him, it was his problem. She had an opportunity to finally do what she'd dreamed of achieving, and Angus Alexander wasn't going to interfere with that.

Pippa let out a sharp whistle above the loud conversations. 'Quiet, everyone, I have some announcements to make.'

Cherry looked over at Pippa. There was no doubt that each of the women who owned and worked on this island was very attractive. Pippa was tall, and had the most unusual apricot-coloured hair. Her dress style was individual, and she always looked trendy. And you always knew wherever Pippa was, Rafe was not far behind.

Oh, to be loved like that.

Again Cherry couldn't help her gaze settling on Angus. It was as though there was a magnet drawing her eyes there. Her heartbeat picked up pace, and as though he could sense she was looking, he turned and his eyes locked with hers. It was damn near impossible to look away.

Warmth ran through her and it was the same feeling that she'd had on Lord Howe Island when they'd spent time together. In those early, heady days before Angus had kissed her. Cherry lifted one hand to her lips, and when it was almost there she woke up to herself. What the hell was she dreaming about? Angus had let her down and she wasn't going to kid herself.

She lifted her eyebrows and grimaced at him. She was off duty for an hour, and didn't have to be polite.

'Hey, everyone.' Pippa smiled at the group. 'I just want to have a quick word and give an official welcome to our new staff. We're so happy to have you all at Ma Carmichael's Resort. Welcome to our four newest recruits. Angus, sous chef, Cherry, apprentice chef, and Tess, who's taken up an office traineeship with Nell, and Dylan, who's replacing the irreplaceable Evie. Sorry, to put the pressure on, Dylan, but you sure have some huge boots to fill there.'

Dylan lifted his glass and called out, 'I'll do my best, Pippa. I'm really happy to be a part of the team on the island.' He was a nice-looking guy with a cultured voice, and he looked and sounded more like a professor than a gardener.

Angus stepped forward and spoke. Cherry looked out at the sea as he thanked Pippa for the opportunity of working in the restaurant.

'Suck up,' she thought. 'Whatever happened to his big plans? His boutique steak restaurant.' She stared at the ocean and ignored his voice. That voice that had once sent shivers down her spine. There were a couple of sailboats heading into the bay, and she watched as the sails were pulled down. By the time Cherry turned her attention back, Angus had stepped back, and Pippa was thanking the builders for the great job they were doing.

'At this pace, we'll be completely open by Christmas,' she said. 'And the good news is, the staff accommodation will have been built up the hill by then, and you'll all have decent-sized rooms and air conditioning.' Rafe stood behind her and Pippa looked up at him as he put his arms around her. 'We were going to leave the old house as your communal area and kitchen, but Eliza and I have met with Danny and Renzo this week, and we've decided to add a kitchen and lounge area to the new staff building up the hill. The old kitchen in the house will be refurbished and we'll run a smaller casual restaurant out of there for coffee and light meals. Angus and Cherry, Tam will talk to you about that after the hoo hah of the wedding is over.'

'Hoo hah?' Rafe said. 'Hey, that's my wedding you're talking about.'

Everyone laughed as Pippa looked up at him. The adoration in her eyes was there for all to see, and it sent a pang of jealousy through Cherry.

'I have another announcement too. This has

been top secret and even Tamsin doesn't know. We've decided on the name for the restaurant. I wanted "Jack Smith's" as a dedication to my gorgeous husband-to-be. For those of you who don't know, that's Rafe's pen name. I'm marrying a famous author.'

Cherry looked across at Angus. He looked as surprised as she was. She'd seen Jack Smith books on his bedside table when she'd stayed at his apartment.

'But when I told Rafe what I was planning, he had a better idea.' She grinned at Tamsin. 'Tam, your exclusive high-class restaurant is going to be called "Violet's". After Aunty Vi.'

Tamsin clapped her hands. 'I love it.'

'Okay, everyone. That's all from me. The sun's about to set and we're here to watch it. Have a good night, everyone.'

All eyes turned to the western horizon where the towering clouds were draped in purple. A gold lining edged the cloud above the mountains and Cherry let out a soft sigh. It was a truly beautiful sight.

The conversation was muted as everyone watched the sun sink behind the mountains. When the sun finally disappeared, Gabe, Tamsin's partner, stepped up onto the rocks and took her hand pulling her up beside him.

'Hey guys, while you're all here together we have an announcement to make too.' He put his arm around Tamsin and she grinned up at him, before looking across at Pippa.

'We were going to leave this until after the wedding so we didn't take away from your special day, Pippa, but our news will impact on the operation of the resort.'

Cherry glanced at Tamsin's left hand, but her ring finger was bare.

'You're engaged!' Pippa exclaimed.

Tamsin shook her head.

'Don't tell us you're moving away from the island?' Nell asked, looking worried.

Pippa put her hands to her mouth. 'Oh no, you can't leave.'

Tamsin's smile grew as Gabe put his arms around her. 'No, we're not going anywhere, and no, we're not engaged—yet. I'm really pleased we have Angus and Cherry on board as there are going to be some changes to the catering set up on the island. For a while anyway.'

Pippa frowned and looked a bit put out, but her expression turned to one of glee when Tamsin put her hand on her stomach.

'We're having the first Pentecost Island baby in just under seven months' time.'

'Oh my God.' Pippa squealed and she and

Nell rushed over to Tamsin. Eliza, Evie and Sienna weren't far behind them.

The happiness and joy coming from the friends was palpable, and it was hard not to smile along with them.

It was lovely news and wonderful to see the happiness, but Cherry bit back a sigh. If only Angus wasn't on Pentecost Island, she could have been one hundred percent happy here too. A traineeship, her own quarters, and the opportunity to do what she'd always wanted and on a beautiful tropical island to make it even better.

She jumped as Angus voice whispered close to her ear. 'I'm going back to the kitchen now, feel free to stay here as long as you want.'

Cherry twisted around and got a shock when her cheek almost brushed Angus' skin. He was standing awfully close to her.

'I'll be up there in ten minutes,' she said, taking a step away from him.

'There's no need.' His voice was cold. 'I've done all the prep.'

'Of course you have.' She couldn't help having the last word. Cherry turned away, feeling like a bitch, but she knew when he'd gone. It was as though she had some stupid sixth sense when Angus was around her.

Regretting her outburst, she ignored the

confusion that drilled through her. How could she feel like that when she didn't care one bit for him? The only way to survive working with Angus was not to give into the emotion that took hold of her; the anger and the disappointment that defined her when he was around. And the undeniable attraction that still came from the memories of her time with him. Angus Alexander had broken her heart, and to this day she didn't know why. She closed her eyes and lifted her glass to her lips.

There was nothing she could do about it, apart from put her head down, work hard and put up with him.

She would survive, and she would get her qualification, no matter what it took.

Chapter Eighteen

Angus - Pentecost Island

Angus strode up the path towards the house. He could have stayed the full hour down on the beach, but once the speeches were done, he'd been keen to get away. He might be being paranoid, but he sensed his welcome to the island was a little cooler than Cherry's; he'd been more at ease in the kitchen. Even though the prep was all done, there were a few things he could do towards tonight's meals.

Tamsin's announcement was obviously going to make a difference to him, but it was Cherry's snarky comment that had peed him off, and on which he now focused.

Who the hell did she think she was?

Standing there having the hide to look drop-dead gorgeous and then turn on him when he was simply being courteous.

He'd turned away before he could bite back, as he was sure she wanted him to. That'd be right; make him look bad to achieve her own ends. He wouldn't fall for that again.

The one thing he couldn't figure out was how she'd sucked him in for those six months last year. She'd had that Miss Perfect quiet-and-shy act in action twenty-four seven, when all the time she'd been scheming behind his back. Maybe even the trip to Lord Howe and the "oh I'm scared of flying" had been an act too. If it had been all about Alan Garner, why weren't they together now? They deserved each other.

Next Saturday—the day of the wedding—was his thirtieth birthday and Angus was frustrated that he'd failed to achieve what he'd wanted to do. No chance he was going to get that in the next seven days. His father had been right; maybe he should have stayed at Linden Downs and been the camp cook.

Maybe he would have been happier.

And he could put the blame squarely at the feet of the woman who was now working with him in the new restaurant.

What did Cherry Chilcott have up her sleeve this time?

It was hard enough having her in the kitchen with him, day and night, and trying to function normally, but seeing her there tonight looking so beautiful had sent a pang of unhappiness spiralling though him.

No matter what a deceiving bitch she was, he was still stupidly attracted to her, even knowing what she was like.

He pushed open the door of the kitchen and

stood in the doorway pushing the heels of his hands into his eyes.

Maybe it was time to think about moving home.

***

After congratulating Tamsin, Cherry walked slowly back to the kitchen. Dylan, the new gardener was sitting on a seat in one of the small forest glades that the paths wound through. Tiny solar lights in the garden lit the path. She stopped when she came level with the seat. 'Hello. We haven't met yet. I'm Cherry. I work in the kitchen.'

He stood and held his hand out. 'Hi, as you've probably guessed, I'm Dylan.'

'Yes, I did. There's more women on the island than men, and I've met the others.'

'A veritable tribe of Amazons from what I'd heard about the place when I applied for the job. Pentecost Island and its unique character is the talk of the coast. Plus the rate it's developing is amazing. You've only just arrived too?'

'Yes, last week.'

'Settled in?'

'Pretty much. How about you?'

'Yes,' he said. 'It's a beautiful place and I'm looking forward to starting work. Evie's done an incredible job in only a few months. Like Pippa said

188

I've got big shoes to fill, plus the next week is busy getting the grounds ready for the wedding. The only thing I'm worried about is the weather holding. Those clouds on the mainland looked a bit ominous before.'

'You don't need to worry about that. The sunsets are like that most afternoons. Those clouds build and then go. I've been over on Hamo for a year, and I reckon the weather will hold until the wedding.'

'I'm not used to the tropics at all, so I'll have to come to you for weather advice.'

'Where are you from?'

'Melbourne, via the UK. I was working on an estate in Cornwall.'

'Wow, that's a huge change.' She was surprised that he'd got the job coming from different climate zones.

Dylan chuckled. 'I can read your mind. Don't worry I know my stuff and there is the Gulf Stream in Cornwall.'

Cherry blushed and dropped her gaze. 'I'm sure you do. Anyway I have to get back to work. Dinner must go on. There are guests waiting.'

'Good to meet you, Cherry.'

'Likewise, I'm sure we'll see each other around. It's not a huge place.' With a wave, she headed back to the house.

Chapter Nineteen

Cherry

Angus was waiting on the veranda and gave her a look that was hard to read, but he didn't comment. She walked past him to her room to get changed. When she entered the kitchen, he had the gas cookers on and was stirring a sauce that smelled delectable.

'We've got some time before the first orders come in, would you like to see how to make the next sauce I'm preparing for tonight? You might as well start learning.'

Cherry hid her surprise; while the question was work-related, Angus' tone was more relaxed than it had been all week.

'Yes, please.' She crossed to the stove, and it was impossible to keep her distance as he reached past her to the bench top behind them as he assembled the ingredients.

'What's that one I can smell? Tomato-based.'

'Yes, that's a pizzaiola sauce. It's a basic basil and tomato mix with a couple of secret ingredients.'

'And this one?' She pointed to the

ingredients on the counter as he leaned across.

Angus glanced at her as his hand brushed her arm. 'Sorry. It's a butter-based sauce with horseradish, Dijon mustard, garlic, chives, shallot, fresh thyme, a pinch of cayenne, salt and pepper. It's not cooked. You only melt the butter and add the rest.'

'That's a great herb garden that Evie planted out near that back shed.'

He nodded. Maybe that was too social a comment, but she realised he was focused on making the sauce when he replied. 'You melt the butter and whisk everything together in a bowl. I find the secret is letting the butter cool marginally before you add everything else.'

'You don't cook the garlic at all?'

'No, but I make sure it's scored all over to let the flavour out.'

It was strange to be having a conversation with Angus. She stood beside him and watched as he whisked the ingredients into the butter. The movement released the aromatic fragrance of the thyme and the garlic.

'It smells divine,' Cherry commented as Angus put the small ceramic bowl aside. 'I would have thought that it was more a white meat sauce.'

He shrugged. 'Personal preference.'

'Is it one you created for when—' Cherry

cut off what she was going to say. For when he had his own place. She wondered why he'd decided against it. A conversation like that was getting into the personal arena.

His eyes narrowed as he looked up at her. 'I'd like you to know that anything I teach you here that is my creation stays in this establishment only. Any dishes I teach you are not for sharing.'

Cherry's stare was as icy as her words. 'That goes without saying. You can trust me.'

The sound he made in reply was a cross between a snort and a pfft. Whatever it was supposed to imply, it was rude.

'Don't speak to me like that please.' One thing Cherry had learned over the past eighteen months was to stand up for herself when she had to.

'I didn't say anything to you.' Angus straightened his shoulders.

'No, but you made a rude noise.'

He shrugged and turned away.'

'Stop it.' Cherry couldn't help the cry that came from her mouth. 'Just stop it, Angus. Don't treat me with disrespect and don't treat me like a fool.'

The door creaked open and Cherry was dismayed to see Tamsin standing there.

'Are you two at it again?' she said. 'Angus?'

'No. I've been showing Cherry how to make

a couple of steak sauces.'

Tamsin looked from Angus to Cherry and back again. 'Is that correct, Cherry?'

She almost felt sorry for Angus as colour ran up his neck; hopefully he'd learn to stop baiting her. Although who knew what it would be like when Tamsin stopped working.

'Yes, that's right,' she said moving back to her work area.

'Have you written the specials board up yet?' Tamsin asked.

Cherry had forgotten and was about to say she hadn't when Angus replied for her. 'We were waiting to see which sauce we'd feature as the special tonight. So we'll go with the thyme and garlic, Cherry, so you can write the board up now.'

Cherry nodded and headed out to the veranda. One minute Angus was being rude to her, and the next he'd made her look good in front of Tam. She'd been quite willing to say that she'd forgotten.

What was it with him? He was doing her head in and they had only just started working together. All she knew was that they couldn't continue like this, and she wasn't going to risk her traineeship. If he kept goading her, and Tam witnessed it again, her traineeship could be at risk. As she wiped the board clean ready to write up the

Friday night specials, Cherry decided it was time to have it out with him once and for all.

Chapter Twenty

Angus

When Tamsin came back into the kitchen during evening service, both Angus and Cherry were exceedingly polite to each other. It was back to "plate up, please" and "heat the sauce" comments only, and they kept their distance from each other. As much as they could in that kitchen anyway.

Once Angus got back into the swing of cooking meals as Mirabelle brought the orders in, it was easier, but he was still aware of Cherry and where she was every second, as well as Tamsin paying close attention to them as they worked.

Finally the last dessert went out, and he relaxed as Tamsin pulled off her apron. 'I'll leave you two to clean up. See you both in here in the morning ready for the move. I told Pippa we'll to work out what stays and what goes. We have to iron out any kinks before the wedding reception.

'Okay,' he said. 'Eight o'clock.'

'Goodnight, Tamsin,' Cherry said.

'Try to stay civil to each other when I leave.' Tamsin looked at them both as she went out the door.

The only sound for the next half hour was

the cool room door creaking open and shut, and water running in the sink. Angus was looking forward to less of the cleaning work when the new kitchen hands started work next week.

He was wiping down the sink when he became aware of Cherry standing behind him. He turned around and caught a strange expression on her face. For a brief moment, it was like when they were together and he had to fight reaching out for her. She'd fitted into his arms perfectly, and he'd love slipping his hands into her hair and releasing that silky curtain of black hair so that it tumbled down to her waist.

He threw the wet cloth into the sink and jammed his hands into his pockets. His tone was harsher than he'd intended. 'What?'

Cherry lifted her chin. 'I want to talk to you.'

'What about?'

'No, not here. Come for a walk to the beach when we're done.'

'Why? What's wrong with here?' Angus knew he was being pig-headed, but the last thing he wanted was to be on a moonlit beach with her. Hell, it was hard enough not touching her in the kitchen.

'There's no knives on the beach.' The corners of Cherry's mouth lifted in a small smile and he knew she was joking. But it reminded him of the old Cherry, the one he'd loved before she'd betrayed him.

'That's not amusing.'

'Oh, for goodness sake, Angus. Just chill a bit, will you? You were never this pig-headed before.'

'And you were never this pushy before.'

'It's not pushy, it's called standing up for myself. Something I was never very good at before, but I have you to thank for that now.'

'Give me a break.'

Her eyes were wide and it was killing him not to touch her.

Shit, he was in trouble here. 'I was going to have an early night.'

'Just humour me, okay? It might do you a favour too. Tam was watching us both closely tonight. I'd suggest if you want to keep your job here—and I know I want to keep mine—that you come down to the beach and we sort this out once and for all.'

'Give me half an hour.'

'Good, I'm pleased you can see sense. I'll meet you down at the rocks where they had the drinks this afternoon.'

Chapter Twenty-One

Cherry

Cherry's bravado disappeared the instant she stepped out of the kitchen. Her knees were shaking as she hurried back to her room. Not only because she'd stood up to Angus, but because he'd agreed to meet her on the beach.

It was hard enough trying to plan what she was going to say, without thinking about being in the dark alone with him. Her fingers felt all light and funny, and her heart was pounding. She paused on the veranda for a few minutes trying to cool down after working in the hot kitchen. The slight breeze off the bay was warm and humid, and she wondered if Dylan was right and the good weather was going to break.

Stepping into her room, she pulled her work clothes off and went to slip on the dress she'd worn earlier when she got a whiff of garlic sauce from her skin. Cherry grabbed her towel and headed for the bathroom. He'd said half an hour so she had time to have her shower, and then she could go straight to bed after talking to him. There was another big day tomorrow with the move and Saturday night was supposed to be busy with yachties in for dinner.

Coiling her hair up on her head so it didn't get too wet, she stood under the shower, and let the hot water wash away her stress and nerves.

It was only Angus, and if she could convince him tonight to be civil in and out of the kitchen, perhaps they could even be friends again. It was time to clear the air. In the months after he'd left her, she'd tried over and over again to figure out what she'd done to make him so angry. The clue appeared to be in his words when they'd met in the kitchen here a week ago.

Lazy. Incompetent. Dishonest.

To the best of her knowledge she was none of those things, and Cherry wondered why he'd used those exact words. With a rueful grin, she thought back to the altercation, and knew that she'd exaggerated too. She'd pretty much implied that he was going to stab her. It had been a heated, irrational altercation where they'd both let their hurt drive them.

But he'd caused that hurt, so he had no reason to accuse her of anything.

Good, she thought as she went back to her room and dressed. Let a little bit of anger build. Think how much he hurt you. Remember those days and nights of crying jags and red wine when your self-worth hit rock bottom.

Remember how he left you with *no good*

reason or explanation.

By the time Cherry had brushed her hair and tied it back, and slipped her sandals on, she was fired up. Her nerves had fled, and she strode down to the beach, thinking about what she was going to say.

Angus was sitting on a rock staring out over the sea. The moon was high and the water held a milky translucence.

'Right,' she said without any hesitation when she reached him. 'It's time to have this out once and for all.'

His head flew around and the moonlight was bright enough for her to see his eyes widen. 'Have it out?' His voice held caution, but she ignored the warning tone.

'Yes. I want to keep my job here. And I guess you do too. Am I correct?'

'Yes, you are correct.'

'So, we need to sort out whatever it is that is making you so pissed off, so we can work together amicably without me worrying every time you pick up a knife in the kitchen.'

'Don't be bloody ridiculous. You know I'd never hurt you, no matter what you did. Although if we're going to be honest, I felt like it for a while back then.'

'Back when? Last Saturday night?'

'No. Last year.'

'Ah ha! Now we're getting somewhere.' Adrenaline raced through Cherry's bloodstream and courage filled her as she stood and faced him. 'Tell me how you could kiss me goodbye three times one morning before you left for work, and then the next day treat me like a piece of dirt beneath your shoe.'

'I caught you out, Cherry. And Garner told me that you'd told him everything.'

She stared at him 'Caught me out? Doing what? I have no idea what you're talking about. And who's Garner?'

'Don't lie to me. You want us to work together, and you want me to tell you the truth. How about you be truthful too? You sold me out. I have no idea how long you were seeing him for. Maybe you knew him before Lord Howe. And for the life of me I never figured out why you did it. I know he hated me. He always did, ever since I won an award that he thought was his.' Angus' voice dropped low as he shook his head. 'Why, Cherry? Just tell me why and maybe we can move forward. You knew it was my dream. I thought you loved me, but there was obviously some other motivation there.'

Cherry couldn't help herself. He sounded so upset, it was breaking her heart. Without thinking she reached out and took his hands in hers. 'Angus. Listen to me. I have absolutely no idea what you're talking about. I don't know any Garners.'

His voice held bitterness and he gripped her hands. 'Don't lie to me. I saw you with him in the bar, and I waited until you came out. But he came out by himself and when I confronted him and told him I knew it was you who'd told him, he laughed and told me I was right. "His pretty little singing waitress", he said.'

Exasperation filled Cherry. 'Have you lost the plot, Angus? I'm still no closer to understanding what or who you're talking about.'

'When I went to work after I left your apartment that morning Garner met me outside Surfside and offered me a job. A job in his new restaurant called AA's using my concept. He said he could help me improve in the business. He didn't mention you until I confronted him after I saw you together that night.'

'Okay, so tell me exactly what you saw and when.'

'I was so pissed off, I needed to talk to you to try to calm down. I thought you understood my dream and I knew that talking to you would help.' His voice held fresh disgust as he obviously relived the night. 'I knocked off early and I went over to Surfside at Surfers, and I walked in looking for you, and what did I see?'

'What did you see?' Embarrassment flooded

through her. Angus had been at the bar and watched her without letting her know. As she thought back to that night, she remembered that guy who had been the reason for Mike's warning and the catalyst that had made her quit. A possibility began to gel. 'Tell me exactly what you saw that night.'

'I saw you cosy with a guy in the dark at the end of the bar. You were so close I didn't even realise it was you until I saw your hair. It looked like you were kissing him. If you weren't, you were up pretty bloody close and personal. I waited and then you made him a drink, and then I realised it was Garner. Bloody Alan Garner of all people. I went outside and I waited for you, but he came out and when I confronted him, he told me everything I needed to hear.'

Everything was beginning to make sense now. Cherry fought for calm.

'You said he called me his singing waitress. Think back, Angus, did he ever use my name?'

He stared at her, their hands still gripped together and he took a deep breath as he thought back. 'No, I don't think he did.'

'Because he didn't know me. Oh, Angus, how can I make you believe me? If only you'd told me this last year. I don't know Alan Garner. What I do know is that a sleazebag grabbed my arm at the bar that night and wouldn't let me go. When you saw us, as you obviously did, he was making a whole slew of filthy suggestions to me and I was telling him to let go.'

Angus stared at her and his eyes glinted in the moonlight. 'That sounds like Garner.'

'And even worse, my boss read the wrong thing into what he thought he saw, *me* flirting with the customers and he threatened to dock my pay. I realised that night how much I hated that job; it wasn't me and that's why I never wanted you to see me singing when I made the cocktails.' Her voice shook and a tear spilled down her cheek. 'I went to Mike and I quit and I walked out through the staff entrance. That's why you didn't see me. I went back to my apartment and I waited for you to come home so I could tell you what I'd done and how proud I was that I found the guts to finally stand up for myself.' The tears on her cheek shone in the moonlight. 'But you never came home, and I never got to tell you what I did.'

Chapter Twenty-Two

Angus

Angus looked down at Cherry's hands in his as he processed what she'd said. 'You don't know him? You really don't know him?'

'No.' Her words were shaky and he could feel her hands trembling. 'I wouldn't lie to you. How can I convince you? I don't know him and you never once mentioned him.'

'I couldn't stand him from the day I met him.' He leaned forward and rested his forehead against hers. 'I stuffed up, didn't I?'

Cherry sniffed and he realised she was crying. He let go of her hands and wrapped his arms around her.

'Oh sweetheart, I am so, so sorry. Garner won in the end. I didn't care about losing AA's to him. What I couldn't cope with was what I thought you'd done. I believed the worst of you. I should have given you a chance, it was unforgivable.'

Cherry leaned into him and he buried his face into her neck. 'I never stopped loving you, you know. That's what gave me so much grief. Even believing you were with Garner, I still missed you like crazy. When I came here and saw you, I just went . . . well you saw how I went.'

'And you saw how I reacted. I've never screeched like that before, and I'm still embarrassed.' She lifted her head and looked at him. 'It was meant to be. You didn't know I was here, and I didn't know you were, and yet you still came to an island. I remember what you said to me about Lord Howe Island being too small.' She smiled at him through her tears. 'Pentecost Island is a lot smaller, but you know the best thing?'

'We're both here?' Angus lifted his hands and slipped the tie out of Cherry's hair. Her hair cascaded down her back and he ran his fingers through it.

'Yes, we're both here and we've both got jobs.'

'Can you forgive me? For what I did. It's no excuse but I have a problem with trust, thanks to my dear old dad.'

'But how did this Garner guy know?' she asked. 'Who else knew your plans?'

'I only ever told one other person, and I'd forgotten because I lost touch with him. A mate called Robbo, and you know what? He played golf with Garner. I never thought of Robbo because Gamer said it was my singing waitress woman who'd told him.'

'Let it go. It doesn't matter in the scheme of

things.' Cherry reached up and held his face tenderly. 'I have . . . or I had . . . a problem with standing up for myself. Thanks to my, not so dear old, dad. If I'd been stronger I would have made sure we had it out then and there, but I was weak. And yes, I love you. Forgiveness goes without saying.'

'We've wasted a lot of time, haven't we, sweetheart?'

'But you know what? I know we've both learned from the experience. And if I'm reading Pippa and Tamsin right, I think you're going to have your own restaurant sooner than you think.'

'Cherry, will you do one thing for me?' Looking into those dark eyes, knowing that she still loved him was the best moment in Angus' life. He knew there were going to be many more.

'What do you want me to do?' she asked huskily as he lowered his head.

'Stop talking and let me kiss you.'

Angus closed his eyes as his lips touched hers.

Chapter Twenty-Three

Pippa

Everyone had come up to our place for dinner after the Friday night drinks. By everyone, I mean the original crew and their partners. Tamsin and Gabe, Nell and Nat, Eliza and Phillipe, Sienna, and Evie and Jed.

Tam and Gabe's news had left us in shock, but we were all really excited for them. We toasted the new baby—Tam and Nell and I shed a happy tear in private, and there was a great deal of laughter and happy talk. There were a few yachts moored in the bay, and music drifted across the water up the hill. The usual warm breeze blew in from the bay, and we sat chatting until late. Most of the others left after coffee but Tam and Nell stayed chatting. As we sat out in the garden after dinner, we could see a few couples from the resort walking back to their huts from the restaurant.

'Looks like there was no bloodshed in the restaurant and the guests were fed,' I said.

Tam rolled her eyes. 'They've survived another night, thank God.'

Rafe's phone buzzed and he apologised and headed inside.

'I'll walk down with the girls,' I called after him.

He waved an acknowledgement.

'So tell me your plans for the restaurant. I assume you're going to take some time off,' I asked Tam as we headed down the hill.

'Angus is a really, really top-class chef. I'll have no hesitation handing over to him if he can commit to a year or two with us.'

'What about the Cherry situation?'

'Whatever it is I think it's building to a head. They've obviously got a past. Before you offer him the head chef position, I'll sit him down and cut to the chase. Tell him what's expected.'

We reached the path at the bottom of the hill and I held my arms open to Tam. 'Give us a hug, Mama. I am so, so happy for you. I still can't believe it.'

I went to hug Nell goodnight before I headed up the hill, but she was staring down at the beach. 'I think your restaurant problem's sorted itself out, Tam.'

She pointed to the beach and we both followed the direction of her finger.

'Yes!' Tam almost squealed with excitement and Nell and I smiled.

Angus and Cherry were walking back to the house, arms around each other and heads close.

Every few steps, they stopped and kissed.

'Aw,' Tam said. 'How gorgeous is that.'

'What a wonderful day,' Nell said.

I walked back up the hill feeling very content.

Epilogue

The night before I married Rafe, I moved out of his house and slept down at Aunty Vi's house. Gabe and Nat had gone up to sleep at Rafe's, so it was a girls only night. It was like old times, if you could call a year ago old times. Nell and Tam and I stayed up late, chatting and reminiscing.

'Might as well act like teenagers again for a while. You're going to be an old married woman this time tomorrow,' Nell said with a giggle.

'Seriously, Pip, are you sure this is right for you? Are you happy?' Tam had always been the worrier of the three of us, and because she was pregnant, tonight she was drinking soda water and wasn't tiddly like Nell and I were.

'I am. I wouldn't change tomorrow for the world.'

'No Darren or Eric regrets?' Tam was persistent.

Nell nudged my shoulder and I spilled my champagne on the old comfy sofa.

'Remember what Aunty Vi used to say to me?' I said mopping at the spilled drink. 'Positivity, Pip? Well, you know what? I'm so certain of Rafe, I don't even need to say or think that anymore. I've

211

found the love of my life. And I trust him. I know he would never hurt me.'

Tam put her head back and sipped her soda water. 'I never dreamed in a million years that the resort would go like this. I remember when we met you in *Solaris* that afternoon and you read the letter from that solicitor, Mr Morton. We imagined we'd be letting out rooms in Aunty Vi's old house to backpackers but, holy shit girls, look at us now!'

'We've done good,' Nell said.

'And we've worked hard too.' I grinned at Tam. 'Just as well you saved Eliza from drowning.'

'And just as well Sienna came to visit,' Tam replied.

'We've got a great team.' Nell giggled again. 'Just as well you didn't turn Evie back when you saw that pink sail.'

'I've got over my pink phobia. Those days are long gone.'

'Please don't tell me your top secret wedding dress is pink!' Nell wagged her finger at me, and I laughed when she almost slid off the sofa

'It's all right for you pair, on the bubbles, and giggling. If I drink any more soda water, I'll be up to the loo all night.' Tam yawned. 'I'm going to bed. I can't get over how much more sleep I need now.'

Nell hiccupped. 'Well, you're sleeping for

two now.'

'Not sleeping, dill.' Tam rolled her eyes. 'That's eating for two, and boy, I'm doing that too.'

I pushed myself up off the sofa. 'Before you go to bed, come down to the beach with me and look at the moon? My last time as a single woman.' I was feeling a little bit emotional. Maybe it was too much champagne, or maybe it was the thought of change.

'A group hug by moonlight,' Nell said as we left the house. Together we walked along the path without speaking and crossed the beach, each of us knowing which rock we were heading for. The moon was full and hung heavy above us. The night sky held a tinge of pink and the brisk wind had whipped up small waves on the usually calm passage. We sat side by side on the edge of the wide flat rock appreciating our close friendship.

'Everything's changing, isn't it?' I said, a little bit maudlin.

'But would you really want it to go back to the way it was?' Nell asked. 'Just for one hour, I'd like to go back and see Aunty Vi in her house and tell her how it was going to be.'

'I know she'd be happy, Pip, and that's what you have to hold close.'

I was sitting in the middle, and Tam reached over and put her arm around my shoulder and then

Nell did from the other side.

'Make me a promise, girls. No matter what happens, we're still—'

'All for one, and one for all,' we chanted together.

***

Surprisingly I slept like a dream. Being back in the old house with Nell and Tam was different, but good. The morning passed quickly as I helped Nell in the office, and Tam went across to the new kitchen to see if Angus and Cherry needed any help.

She brought lunch back to the house for us and we sat on the veranda. The casual chefs were already in the kitchen here where the inhouse guests would be served dinner tonight as the wedding reception took over the new restaurant and bar.

'No champagne until we go down to Sienna and the day spa,' I said as Tam put a platter of meat and cheese on the table. 'I was floating when she did the practice run last week.'

'Is your dress down there already?' Tam asked.

I nodded. 'Sienna and Evie had a sneak peek so they could get the makeup and the hair right.'

'Ooh, I can't wait,' Nell said.

'Not long now.' I smiled.

When we'd finished lunch, Tam headed for her shower, and Nell went to answer the phone.

I waited on the veranda for the girls to walk down to the day spa with me. It was a brilliant Whitsundays day; the sky and the water were such a brilliant blue you could barely see the horizon. Serenity filled me and I let out a soft sigh.

The noise of a boat motor easing back caught my attention and I turned to look at our bay, and was surprised to see Jiminy's boat approaching the wharf. He and his wife, Sarah were guests at the wedding but they were arriving very early.

Rafe came running down the steps from his house towards the wharf. A tall slim woman in white stepped off Jiminy's boat as he tied it up.

I frowned. It wasn't Sarah and to my knowledge there were no new guests coming in today. We'd cleared the bookings calendar for the wedding day. The only guests in-house were those who were already here.

Rafe stepped onto the wharf, and the woman clutched her broad-brimmed white hat as she ran down and clung to him. His arms went around her and his dark head rested against hers for a long time. A very long time.

A few moments later, a couple stepped onto the wharf.

Then it hit me. These were Rafe's publisher friends and their daughter, Odessa. Why hadn't Rafe told me they were arriving today?

'What are you looking so glum about?' Tam stood beside me, her hair wrapped in a towel. I pointed to the wharf. 'We have unexpected guests.'

Tam peered past me. 'Who?'

'I know I'm being a bitch, but why the hell did *she* have to arrive today of all days? On our wedding day!'

'Who? Who is it, Pip?' Tam put her hand on my shoulder and I took a deep breath.

'A friend of Rafe's from England. We were expecting her, but not yet. Or at least I wasn't. She's had a horrible tragedy in her life, and she was coming here to get over it. Her parents are here too. They own the company that publishes Rafe's books.'

'As guests, or staying at your place?'

I shrugged. 'I don't know. I'm right out of the English friend loop.'

'Well, I'll go and see Nell right now, and see what huts are free, because they can't stay with you and Rafe tonight. It's your wedding night, for goodness sake.'

'I know,' I said glumly. And more to the point, why hadn't Rafe told me *she* was arriving? I thought. He must have known that she, I mean, they were arriving, I told myself. All I could think of, was the way that Odessa had clung to him.

'Are you ready, girls?'

With a forced smile I turned to Sienna as she walked up the stairs.

'Hello, my lovely, the day spa awaits you.'

As I walked through the dim forest with Sienna and Tam, to get ready for our wedding, my serenity was tainted by a niggling doubt.

THE END

Will Pippa and Rafe's wedding go ahead as planned?

Are you ready for the next Pentecost Island story?

Odessa Walker can't remember the last time she felt safe. Her recovery after an accident on a motorway outside London is fraught with difficulty. Her physical rehabilitation is successful, but her accident has had a significant impact on her mental health. Her parents, Jenny and Bryant, Rafe's publishers, have asked if Odessa can come to Pentecost Island to hasten her recovery, and hopefully restore her confidence. Pippa readily agrees, but the new arrival creates tension, not only between Pippa and Rafe, but also within the friendship group of the women on the island.

Dylan Nash has replaced Evie Stephenson as head landscaper on Pentecost Island. His first encounter with Odessa is confronting, and when

Dylan attempts to make amends for the misunderstanding, she refuses to accept his apology.

Odessa's presence changes the friendships in the close-knit community on the island. Will Dylan's gentle nature, and his attraction to Odessa, help her regain her confidence, or will his determination compromise her recovery?

Odessa is available for pre-order at:

https://www.annieseaton.net/store.html

Also by Annie Seaton

Click on each title to see more details

Signed copies available from Annie's online store
in print
https://www.annieseaton.net/store.html

Whitsunday Dawn

Undara

Porter Sisters Series

Kakadu Sunset

Daintree

Diamond Sky

Hidden Valley (2021)

Pentecost Island Series (2020)

Pippa

Eliza

Nell

Tamsin

Evie

Cherry

Odessa

Sienna

Tess

Isla

Bondi Beach Love Series

Beach House

Beach Music

Beach Walk

Beach Dreams

Second Chance Bay Series

Her Outback Playboy

Her Outback Protector

Her Outback Haven

Her Outback Paradise

Love Across Time Series

Come Back to Me

Follow Me

Finding Home

(November 2020)

The Threads that Bind

(2021)

The Trouble with Paradise

Deadly Secrets

Adventures in Time

Silver Valley Witch

The Emerald Necklace

Worth the Wait

Acknowledgements

A special thank you to my wonderful editor and critique partner, Susanne Bellamy, and my eagle-eyed proof-readers, Roby Aiken, Nicki Edwards, Anna Welch and Kristen Woolgar.

About the Author

AWARDS

2014 - Author of the Year Ausrom Readers' Choice

2015 - Best Established Author Ausrom Readers' Choice

2016 - Finalist for Author of the Year, Book of the Year, Cover of the Year, Ausrom Readers' Choice

2016 – Finalist RWA Ruby Award: Kakadu Sunset-

2017 - Best Established Author, Ausrom Readers' Choice

2018 - Finalist NZ KORU Award: Her Outback Cowboy

2018 Book of the Year (Whitsunday Dawn) Ausrom Readers' Choice Awards

2019 - Finalist NZ KORU Award: Her Outback Haven

Annie lives in Australia, on the beautiful north coast of New South Wales. She sits in her writing chair and looks out over the tranquil Pacific Ocean. She has fulfilled her lifelong dream of becoming an author and is producing books at a prolific rate.

She writes contemporary romance and loves telling

the stories that always have a happily ever after. She lives with her very own hero of many years and they share their home with Toby, the naughtiest dog in the universe, and Barney, the rag doll kitten, who hides when the grandchildren come to visit.

Stay up to date with her latest releases at her website: **http://www.annieseaton.net**

If you would like to stay up to date with Annie's releases, subscribe to her newsletter on her website.